The Great Event

A sequel to
The WARNING

by
John M. Haffert

Nihil Obstat

In keeping with the decree of the Congregation for the Propagation of the Faith, A.A.S., 58, 1186, the publishers have exercised due care that there is nothing herein contrary to faith or morals and further declare that in all matters, and in all reference to alleged miracles or private revelations, they submit to the final and official judgment of the Magisterium of the Church.

Copyright by John M. Haffert, January 2000

Distributed in the U.S.A. by:
The 101 Foundation, Inc.
P.O. Box 151
Asbury, NJ 08802
Phone: (908) 689-8792
Fax: (908) 689-1957
www.101foundation.com
e-mail: 101@101foundation.com

ISBN: 1-890137-42-1

CONTENTS

Chapter	Page
FOREWORD	
LET THE TRIUMPH BEGIN	v
INTRODUCTION	
WALLS COME DOWN	vii
Twelve stars of the Woman of the Apocalypse at the borders of fifteen nations	
1 COMING: THE GREAT EVENT	1
Foretold by Saints — Coming Soon	
2 WAITING	5
What is going to happen?	
3 NOW MOST URGENT	13
"Nearing its fulfillment." –Pope John Paul II	
4 "ONCE WAS MARY"	19
Her power and Her Royalty	
5 MIRACLE OF BLOOD	25
More than a miracle is needed to change the world	
6 MIRACLE OF FATIMA UNVEILS THE FUTURE	33
They cried their sins aloud and prayed for mercy	
7 THE GREAT EVENT	40
Seeing ourselves as God sees us	
8 THE TRIUMPH	46
It is certain. It has begun.	

9 TO HASTEN THE TRIUMPH 52
   What has been delayed can be hastened!

10 CONSECRATION TO THE
   IMMACULATE HEART 60
   The most important decision

11 THE ERA OF PEACE 69
   The most important condition

12 PERSONAL TRIUMPH 73
   Already begun in the hearts of many

13 MAKE IT KNOWN 84
   "Mobilize the Laity"

14 APPEAL TO PRIESTS 93
   God does not want Her in the
   background now.

15 QUEEN WITH PRAYING HANDS 101
   An answer for those who doubt

16 HELP FROM HEAVEN 108
   "I will cooperate then in a different way."

17 TRIUMPH NOW 113
   So many changes from 1985 to 2000!

18 WHAT WILL THE TRIUMPH BE? 119
   "A new springtime of Christianity"
   –Pope John Paul II

19 THE FIRST STEP TO VICTORY 127
   Place the hearts of millions in
   Our Lady's Heart

AFTERWORD
   TWO CROWNS 133
   The prophecies and signs of the Triumph

FOREWORD

LET THE TRIUMPH BEGIN

The title of this book was intended to be: *Let the Triumph Begin!* Those words will appear time and again in these pages. But essentially, this book is about a predicted great intervention of God, which will be experienced by each and every person on earth. This great event will be an act of God's Mercy. It may be mankind's last chance to avoid a universal chastisement.

Fifteen years before this present book, I had worked with a saintly Passionist priest, Rev. Philip Bebie, on a little book called *The Warning*. Principal parts of that little book are quoted in this one. The quotations are indented, not quite as wide as the rest of the text.

To Avoid Confusion

It is important to note this because while I speak in this book of the Great Event as not yet having taken place, the little book written fifteen years ago (the quotes from which are indented) was intended to be read only AFTER the Great Event had taken place. *Those parts speak of the event as though it had just happened.*

While dying of cancer, Father Bebie wrote most of it himself in the very last days of his life. Much of what he wrote then seems now almost prophetic.

The original little book, *The Warning* (from which only parts are quoted here) is available from the 101 Foundation.

Please Read All

It is important to read the *Introduction* to this present book, and the *Afterword*. Both speak of signs of the Triumph having already begun.

The *Afterword* speaks also of other prophecies concerning the alternative to the world's failure to respond to the great event. It reminds us of the powerful words of Pope John Paul II in his October 13, 1997 letter to the bishop of Fatima—that the importance of Fatima is not so much in the supernatural events but that we are now given *the specific response needed* to meet *the alternative of "mankind's self-destruction."*

Also in the *Afterword* is an explanation of the front and back cover designs of this book.

I was privileged to collaborate with Father Bebie in writing about "The Great Event" fifteen years before the new millennium. We have seen amazing changes in those fifteen years!

I am sure his hand is in these pages you are now about to read.

INTRODUCTION

WALLS COME DOWN

Twelve stars of the Woman of the Apocalypse at the borders of fifteen nations

The fallen Berlin Wall was a symbol not only of a once-divided nation but of a divided world. Part of that wall now stands at one of the entrances of the sanctuary of Fatima where, in an apparition to three children, the Queen of the World promised "an era of peace for mankind."

Many other less visible but real walls between nations of Europe have crumbled almost without notice. *Walls dividing fifteen nations*, which were previously open only at "points of entry," *are no longer there.*

These many walls existed between Great Britain and the continent, between France and Germany, Spain and Portugal, France and Italy, down the entire list of most nations of the entire world including the United States, which even today can be legally entered only by proof of citizenship or presentation of a valid visa and a declaration of one's possessions, subject to search and tariff.

Severe Division

The divisions in Europe were particularly severe in the century just passed. Two wars had set nation against nation after taking a toll of millions of European lives. The heavily armed Maginot line, with fortresses, bunkers, mine fields, and trenches, separated France from Germany. Some borders, like the one between France and Spain in 1947, which had been closed because of French interference in the Spanish civil war, were at times impassable.

It must be difficult for present day travelers in Europe to realize what it was like *just those few years ago* when its nations lived in fear of neighbors. In a way, it is sad that many reading these lines will not remember. *They will not be able fully to realize what an amazing change has taken place.*

The Triumph promised at Fatima has begun. And soon, we expect a Great Event which will change the entire world.

Border "Walls"

This writer began to travel to Europe and the Middle East in 1946 to promote the World Apostolate of Fatima (the Blue Army). Pages had to be added to his passport, long before it expired, to accommodate all the visas required at border crossings. When the world peace flights began with the famous Pilgrim Virgin statue, "visas" had to be obtained even to fly over many of the nations of the world. Personal contact had to be made with the president of Egypt for a direct flight to Tel Aviv after Israel agreed. *It was the first civilian flight in history between the two nations.*

Permission even to overfly vast parts of the world, as in China and Russia, were rarely given. The Queen of the World plane, carrying the Pilgrim Virgin, also made the first-ever civilian flight from the Soviet Union to Berlin before the destruction of the wall. Now, with frequent flights taken for granted, the time when any flight was impossible without danger of the plane being shot down from the sky seems remote.

There was the time when Czechoslovakia agreed to let a group pass into Poland, but Poland would not open the gates on the other side of the bridge. It was the millennium of Christianity in Poland and the Pope had been refused a visa.

The special plane (a Boeing 707) bore on its side in large letters: *Queen of the World*. It was used for "Peace Flights," which set several precedents, such as the first civilian flight ever to take place from Egypt to Israel. Another was the first passenger chartered flight ever to take place around the entire world. Another was the first direct civilian flight between the Soviet Union and the free city of Berlin. It carried the Pilgrim Virgin to many nations, including a circle flight around the entire continent of Africa, with the message and the hope of Our Lady's great promise: *An era of peace for mankind.*

There were so many visas, so many troublesome border crossings. Sometimes a wait at a border might take a day or more until a visa cleared.

So had it been throughout almost the entire world, with greater or less intensity, for thousands of years.

Miraculous Change

One of the major "documents" for tracing the life of St. Benedict Joseph Labré at the time of his canonization was the large accumulation of visas from his many pilgrimages. They were often not only between nations but between one duchy and the next, one province and another.

Was there any reason to suppose any of this would change? These walls had existed for centuries. Could we expect them to come down, like the Berlin Wall, before the third millennium?

Could we expect them to come down before the end of the bloodiest century in history, especially in Europe where, in that century, millions had been slaughtered in two international wars?

The Seeminigly Impossible

But the change came, sometimes dramatically as with the fall of the Berlin Wall, sometimes almost miraculously, as when the Pilgrim Virgin statue of Our Lady of Fatima opened the border between Spain and France in 1947.*

The statue had left Fatima two months before to be taken *processionally* across Europe to Russia. That

---

* A congress of youth at Fatima in 1947 resolved that a statue of Our Lady of Fatima be carried processionally to Russia. One statue set forth in May in an easterly direction, and a second in October in a westerly direction. Wonders occurred along the way. Pope Pius XII said in 1951: "I crowned Our Lady of Fatima Queen of the World in 1946, and the following year, She set forth *as the Pilgrim Virgin, as though to claim Her dominion.*"

Pilgrim Statue of Our Lady of Fatima crossing the frontier from Spain to France in July, 1947. Notice crowds on rooftops in background. Newspapers reported some two hundred thousand gathered on the two sides of this border which had been closed for more than ten years and which opened in the path of Our Lady.

meant it had to be *carried*. When it arrived at the border of France, the frontier was closed to all traffic because of French involvement in the Spanish Civil War.

Thousands of people gathered on both sides of the border because of wonders which had occurred along the path of the statue ever since it had departed from Fatima. In Valladolid, just a week earlier, tens of thousands had lined the streets when the statue passed. The crowds jammed the square where the statue stopped for a short time and a woman, with a seventeen-year-old deaf-mute daughter, began to work her way through the crowd, leading her daughter towards the statue. The girl had been deaf and mute since infancy.

Slowly, the woman pressed her way through the crowd. Some who knew her, and others who read the years of mingled pain and hope in her motherly face, parted to let her pass towards the image which had come from Fatima.

When mother and daughter finally came near the statue, the girl (who from infancy had never heard and had never spoken a word) threw up her arms before Our Lady and cried out: *"Holy Virgin! Mother of God!"*

Now, as the statue approached the border, the crowds on the French side were expecting only to see the statue across the barrier because *no permission had been given* to open the gate.

But wonder of wonders, it opened. The border police simply ignored the rules they had followed for over ten years! Shortly afterwards the governments of France and Spain agreed that it remain open.

When the Pilgrim Virgin "opened" the Franco-Spanish border in 1947, there were cries of awe and surprise. But it is difficult to imagine the surprise experienced by frequent international travelers when national barriers crumbled like the Berlin Wall at the end of the century.

Border Surprise!

For years, this writer traveled from time to time from Portugal to Spain via Tuy, where a river separates the two countries. One could expect a major delay (an hour or more) for control of documents and baggage inspection before crossing the narrow bridge over the river.

In 1993, after more than thirty years of this experience, he had his passport ready as he neared the border. To his surprise, there was no border control on the Portuguese side of the bridge. "I guess they are on the other side," he thought, keeping his passport handy.

But there was also no control on the Spanish side! The only sign of leaving the one country and entering the other was *a circle of twelve gold stars on a blue plaque.*

In the middle of the circle of stars on one side of the river was the name *Portugal*, and in the circle of stars on the other side was the name *Spain*. The car continued without a stop from one country to the next, past the blue plaques and circle of stars, *as though the nations on both sides had become one country.*

Even Greater Surprise

One might consider this possible because Portugal and Spain share the same peninsula. They have had their wars through the centuries, but perhaps it should not be such a surprise that they might decide to do away with border controls. But surely now there would be a control for a foreigner, in a foreign car, going from Spain to France.

But surprise of surprises! At the crossing into France at the edge of the Pyrenees, *again there was a blue plaque with twelve stars.* Inside the circle on one side was the name: *Spain.* Inside the circle of twelve stars of an identical plaque on the other side was the name: *France.*

There was no control for foreign car, driver, passengers. *It was as though Spain and France were one country!*

But surely when at the Rhine, to cross from France to Germany, it would be different.

But surprise of surprises! On the French side of the Rhine, the station for passport control was not only closed but the window was cracked and dirty. It was abandoned. It was a deserted building. *Next to it was the blue plaque with the circle of twelve stars.* In the circle: *France.* On the other side of the Rhine, as you sped over the international bridge, in the same circle of twelve stars: *Germany.*

After more than a thousand years, the borders of Europe seemed to have ceased to exist!

The plaques at each border are plaques of *the flag of Europe: a banner of blue with a single circle of twelve stars.* And the greatest surprise of all is that this banner was designed from the Medal of the Immaculate Conception (the "Miraculous" Medal). *The circle of twelve stars symbolize the crown of the Woman of the Apocalypse "crowned with twelve stars."*

Most people even in Europe do not know the amazing reason for the twelve star flag of the European nations.

Abbé Caillon, a theology professor at the major seminary in Caen and a leader of the Blue Army in France, happened to know the man who designed the flag of Europe. Abbé Caillon himself told us that the designer said: *"I was inspired by the twelve stars on the Miraculous Medal, the twelve stars of the crown of the Woman of the Apocalypse."*

The Twelve Stars

St. John describes Her in Chapter 12 of his Book of Revelation:

"A great mysterious sight appeared in the sky...a Woman, whose dress was the sun and who had the moon under her feet and *a crown of twelve stars on her head.* A huge red dragon then appeared, with seven heads and ten horns and a crown on each of his heads. A great battle ensued. Then a great voice was heard: *'Now God has shown His power as King!'* The dragon went after the Woman, *'but the earth helped Her.'"*

At Fatima in 1917, Our Lady asked our help. She asked for our sacrifices and prayers to bring about the conversion of Russia. She promised that if we did as She asked, Russia would be converted and "an era of peace will be granted to mankind."

In confirmation of this promise, *She appeared in the sun,* the fires of which seemed to plummet towards the earth as though to consume all in its path. As the tens of thousands of witnesses cried out for mercy, the fire gathered back into the sky.

There was no doubt that the Woman of the Apocalypse had come to ask the earth to help Her.

First Border Victory

"Ave, Ave, Ave Maria!"

Now there is NO border control. Instead there is the blue plaque with *the circle of the twelve stars,* where the border control used to be.

Those of the century 2000 and beyond might not even be able to imagine the suffering that closed such frontiers in the first place. In 1947, Spain was still reeling from a most devastating civil war, drenched in the blood of hundreds of thousands of her citizens. This writer visited Spain at that time and saw the destruction which rivaled the destruction to be seen in the aftermath of the war in France and Germany. He wrote shortly afterwards, in his 1948 book *Russia Will Be Converted,* almost prophetically:

European Union Flag

"A revolution of Faith, nurtured by the blood of the martyrs, is certain to succeed where a revolution of arms and death did not."

Great Price Has Been Paid

In the ensuing pages, when we speak of the Triumph which has already begun, and which we expect to be unprecedented in the history of the world, let us not forget the price that has been paid.

It is said there are no atheists in foxholes. Millions of those who died in the great European wars of this past century turned to God and offered their lives for peace. Millions also died (especially in Russia and Spain) for their faith.

If we are to be blessed with the "Great Event" described in this book, it is because many died for us, and many have already responded to the words of Our Lady at Fatima: "If people do as I say, many souls will be saved...an era of peace will be granted to mankind."

The first great sign of her victory is at the border crossings of fifteen countries which, at one time or another in this past century, were fighting each other. Another sign is the move of Turkey, a Muslim nation, to embrace this same flag.

And Islam?

Most wars continuing in the new millennium are involved with Islam. This Islamic confrontation with Christianity reached a peak in the 16th century when forces of Islam, under Turkish leaders, stormed the walls of Vienna. Their advance was broken in a victory over the Turkish fleet on October 7, 1571. That day was then designated the Feast of Our Lady of Victory, changed one year later to the Feast of Our Lady of the Rosary.

Islam extremists today menace the Western world with terrorism in a time of increasing availability of atomic weapons.

But the Woman crowned with twelve stars has come in our time. And Archbishop Sheen dared to say that She chose to be known by the name of Fatima, the name of the daughter of Mohammed, because "She came not only for the conversion of Russia but for Islam."*

Who could have imagined, as the new millennium began, that Turkey would be seeking entry into the European union?

The true "surprise of surprises" will be the flag of twelve stars at the border of Turkey—*the sign of the Woman clothed in the sun and promising: "Finally My Immaculate Heart will Triumph. An era of peace will be granted to mankind."*

If so many walls have come down already, what will the world be like after the great intervention of God, which we may now expect?

---

* See the author's books Hand of Fatima *and* God's Final Effort.

CHAPTER ONE

COMING: THE GREAT EVENT!

Foretold by Saints – Expected Soon

In her first appearance on her own Eternal World Television Network, the day after the miraculous cure which enabled her to put aside the steel braces she had worn for over forty years, Mother Angelica was asked in the exuberance of the moment about the future.

She answered by repeating two prophecies which had been made by saints in the past and which seem now close to fulfillment. (The Pope himself had said in his daring book, *Crossing the Threshold of Hope:* "It seems, as we approach the millennium, that the words of Our Lady of Fatima are nearing their fulfillment.")

The first great prophecy Mother Angelica expected to see fulfilled in the near future was that, *on a given day all over the world, people will see themselves as God sees them.*

Blessed Anne Marie Taigi, who prophesied this almost two hundred years ago, called it *a worldwide Illumination of Conscience.* Others have called it a "Warning." We will refer to it as "the Great Event."

The Warning

In 1984, I had collaborated with Father Philip Bebie, C.P., in publishing a little book describing this anticipated Great Event. We called the book *The Warning*, based on the messages of Garabandal.[1] But Garabandal had not yet been approved by local ecclesiastical authority because, even if the Bishop was favorable (which indeed seemed the case), *the Church could not approve an event for which the final proof itself had not yet been given.*

But, since it had also been predicted by St. Edmund Campion and Blessed Anne Marie, we decided to go ahead. To be sure we were doing the right thing, we obtained permission (*nihil obstat*) from Father Bebie's major superior in the Passionist Order.

Father Philip's Insight

Father Philip was a priest with special gifts. He was a founding member of a Passionist House of Solitude. He was administrator of the first two Charismatic priests conferences in Steubenville, Ohio (1975-76). He preached missions until diagnosed with terminal cancer in 1983.

We became friends and collaborators two years before his terminal illness when we cooperated in the publication of his book *Proclaim Her Name.*

---

[1] Garabandal is a village in northwest Spain where Our Lady of Mount Carmel is reported to have appeared to four children. She said She came *"to draw all to Our Hearts."* She predicted an Illumination of Conscience as a warning to the world. It would be followed by a miracle. If the world did not respond, there would be a chastisement. (See *Afterword* at end of this book.)

Father Philip Bebie, speaking into microphone, in a blessing of oil in 1981, the year in which he felt inspired to write about the expected Illumination of Conscience: the "Warning."

He was already suffering the final stages of the disease when *The Warning* (concerning the prophesied Illumination of Conscience) was completed in 1984. He died soon afterwards.

We had both long felt the need to make known this prophesied "Great Event," so that people would understand what was happening when it took place. *It would happen suddenly, and it would happen only once.* Many might despair. It seemed urgent to let the world know what was in store.

This event had already been experienced by various individual persons, such as Estelle Faguette at Pellevoisin[2] and Saint Faustina in Poland. Now it was

---

[2] Estelle Faguette received 15 apparitions of Our Lady in 1876, after the first of which she experienced the Illumination of Conscience. (For more information about the apparitions, which were approved by the Church in 1984, see the author's book *Her Glorious Title.*) Although a devout person who had led an almost blameless life, Estelle felt overcome with grief as she saw herself as God saw her. Other individual persons have had a similar experience. It is now predicted for the entire world.

expected to happen to every man, woman, and child on earth.

It would be a turning point in history.

Would Be Too Late

In his great concern that the world should understand the far-flung implications of the "Warning," or "Illumination of Conscience," Father Bebie's original intention was to prepare an explanation to be disseminated the moment it happened.

I suggested that would be too late.

As the cancer left him daily weaker, he offered all until finally the book was ready. A small number of copies were printed for free distribution using my home post office box as an address.

Now, fifteen years later, at the time of the publication of this book, much of what was written then seems more meaningful. Some of it (especially about the Triumph) seems prophetic. It seems more urgent, especially since the word did not spread as effectively as we thought it would when, because of our own sense of urgency, we offered the books free of charge.

But the word is out. Mother Angelica's announcement took care of that. And someone had the initiative to put the little book on the internet.

In the chapters which follow, we will identify, with an introduction and conclusion, the original words of *The Warning* with minor "update" modifications.

As the reader will see, *events are moving rapidly.*

We now have some important insights not available fifteen years ago when *The Warning* was written. We believe this Great Event will mark a major turning point in history, as did the Great Flood.

CHAPTER TWO

WAITING

What is going to happen?

"What do YOU think is going to happen?" is a question one often hears in this time of expectation. Even though many have definite opinions, most hesitate to reply. How could anyone know enough, even from a lifetime of learning and experience, to say what will happen tomorrow? And how could one discern between truth and speculation among the messages of the many visionaries of our time?

Despite my advanced age, and even though I knew Father Philip Bebie was an enlightened person, I was still hesitating to write this book when I went to Fatima on September 24, 1999, even though I knew in general what I wanted to share with all who are *waiting*.

I felt the same urgency which compelled Father Bebie in the final days before the certain death he knew was rapidly approaching—the urgency to make known the Great Event of which we had written fifteen years ago. More than ever, I felt that if we wait until it happens, *it may be too late to help many who might be overwhelmed by it.*

Many were now saying that the Triumph is at hand. Sister Lucia of Fatima had said recently (October 11, 1993): *"The Triumph is an ongoing process."*

But a desire to share such a message is far from the deed. How should one actually respond to such a challenge? Where should one begin?

After struggling to begin for almost two weeks at Fatima, I decided that, on the Feast of Our Lady of the Holy Rosary (also Our Lady of Victory), I would trust Our Lady to show the way. And, at that very moment, an unusual incident loosed my reluctant pen. It seemed

Statue of Our Lady of the Holy Innocents. The "Mother" holding in Her hands a fetus, praying and offering all the babies of the world slaughtered in their mothers' wombs.

that Our Lady showed the way by actual events which may speak for themselves.

Our Lady of All Nations

Jimmy Williamson, the cofounder of the Queen of the World Center at the Fatima Castle, had commissioned a statue of Our Lady as "Mother of the Innocents." It was a representation of Our Lady gazing to Heaven with tears in Her eyes, holding a fetus.

Shortly after commissioning the statue six months before, Jimmy died. We received notice, on the vigil of the Feast of the Rosary, that the statue was ready. Since I was a trustee of the International Center of the Queen of the World at the Fatima Castle, for which Mr. Williamson had destined this statue of the "Mother of the Innocents," it fell to me to go to the studio to accept it.

To my surprise, next to the new statue of Our Lady of the Innocents, I saw a most beautiful image of Our Lady of All Nations. With the exception of the image of Our Lady of Akita (which was of unpainted wood), I had never seen a statue of Our Lady under this title. I stood before it with surprise and awe. *It was Our Lady of the Triumph.*

To Be Focal Point

We had planned a ceremony the following week (on October 13, 1999) at the International Center of the Queen of the World. It was to be a sort of pre-inauguration of this sanctuary-museum complex built to contain hundreds of statues of Our Lady from all the nations of the world.

October 13 had been chosen for the ceremony because the miracle of the sun, which took place on October 13, 1917, had inspired Pope Pius XII to proclaim and crown Our Lady of Fatima as Queen of the World. This October 13th would be the last anniversary of the miracle before the millennium.

8

At once, we asked if it would be possible to have the statue of Our Lady of All Nations for the inauguration.

Not Possible?

The images of Our Lady of All Nations, and of Our Lady in tears holding a fetus, seemed to express much of what we wanted to say in the Queen of the World Center. They also imaged what I wanted to say in this book. One speaks of the rejection of God by sins of contraception and abortion in all the nations of the

The wood carving of the statue which "came alive" in Akita, Japan was copied from the widely known picture of Our Lady of All Nations. The author had never seen any similar statue until the day he began to write this book.

world; the other speaks of Our Lady standing on the world and flooding it with God's Merciful Love. One speaks of the tidal wave of evil which seems impossible to stem; the other speaks of Her to whom "God has entrusted the peace of the world" (as told to us by Blessed Jacinta), and promises the Triumph of Her Immaculate Heart.

The studio regretfully informed us that our request for the statue of Our Lady of All Nations could not be granted. It had been on order for some months and was about to be sent to Austria.

While we were discussing the details of having a copy made, to our complete surprise the owner of the studio called Austria in the off chance that the person who had commissioned the statue would wait another six months. It turned out that the person in Austria was a member of the Blue Army and, at the mention of my name and the purpose for which the statue was desired, he at once released it.

Little Signs

In little events, Our Lady seemed to be showing the way to write about Her Triumph.

We went to pick up the statue of Our Lady of All Nations on October 12. That night, I awoke in the very early hours of the morning and went to my window facing the Basilica of Fatima. I had slept only a few hours but was wide awake.

Gazing at the illuminated statue of the Immaculate Heart on the facade of the Basilica, in the total silence of the early morning hours, I began to write.

In the Silence

It was not only the vigil of the anniversary of the miracle at Fatima. It was also an important international day of Our Lady—Feast of the Patroness of Spain (Our Lady of the Pillar of Saint James), Feast of the Patroness of the Americas and of the Philippines

(Our Lady of Guadalupe), and Feast of the Patroness of Brazil (Our Lady of Aparecida). She was the Lady of All Nations.

Tens of thousands would shortly be gathering at Fatima for the vigil of the final visions (Saint Joseph and Our Lord also appeared at Fatima on the 13th). This particular October 13, as we have said, was the last anniversary of the Great Miracle before the new millennium.

On this same day in 1947, when the Pilgrim Virgin statue was blessed here in the presence of hundreds of thousands of pilgrims, I had myself seen a major miracle.

In niche on the facade of the Basilica of Fatima is the giant statue of the Immaculate Heart of Mary sculpted by Rev. Thomas McGlynn. This book was begun in the night of October 12 when the author, gazing at the statue illuminated at night, was reminded of witnessing with Father McGlynn the miracle of St. Januarius. It prompted the question: *Would the "Great Event" accomplish what miracles have failed to do?*

In the silence of the night, the pent up thoughts I wanted to share in these pages began to flow.

The World Center

We are told that these are apocalyptic times—the "last times." *A radical change throughout the entire world is expected to take place.* Many holy souls have had bits and pieces of the vision of the Triumph specifically prophesied by Saint Louis Grignion de Montfort over three hundred years ago and now felt to be close.

The saint foretold the great Triumph through Mary. At Fatima, She to whom "God entrusted the peace of the world," promised that Triumph now.

Since making that promise at Fatima in 1917, Our Lady has returned several times with additional messages, several of which have been examined and confirmed by the Church as truly supernatural.

Two of those approved apparitions, one in Holland and one in Japan (Our Lady of Akita carved after a likeness of Our Lady's appearance in Holland) have been of Our Lady of All Nations.[3] In both of those Church-approved apparitions, *Our Lady has given to the world some grave warnings, and a great hope.*

She has spoken of the Triumph and even told us when it will take place.

As I gazed at the Basilica, bathed in spotlights and shining out of the silent black of the night, the giant statue on the facade stood out more than usual because the tower above it was covered with scaffolding and curtains.

---

[3] While the supernatural character of the apparitions of Our Lady of all Nations in Amsterdam was confirmed by the local Ordinary in 1996, there is some question as to whether all aspects of the apparitions and messages have been formally approved. A declaration was made that the seer was of sound mind and worthy of credence.

I never guessed that it would be the day I was writing the last chapter of this book that *I would see what was under those curtains*—a final little sign that Father Philip Bebie had inspired my desire to once again lift the curtain on "the Great Event" as we entered the new millennium.

It was time to say to all who wait: *"Let the Triumph begin."*

This is taken from an actual photograph of a page in a secular publication in Portugal published just after the miracle of the sun. Pictures at top and bottom show that the sun had detached itself to hurtle upon the earth, causing all to think it was the end of the world. Picture at right shows the three children.

CHAPTER THREE

NOW MOST URGENT

"Nearing its fulfillment." –Pope John Paul II

As said above, it was the daily circumstances surrounding the celebration of the anniversary of the miracle of Fatima that finally "loosed my pen." With the indulgence of the reader, for another few moments, I would like to permit events of that anniversary of the Fatima miracle, in which the Holy Father participated from Rome, to continue to speak to us.

I had come to Fatima not to write this book but to finalize some details of the Queen of the World Center where, as mentioned above, images of Our Lady from all nations of the world are assembled as visible witness to Her Queenship and universal Motherhood.

G. K. Chesterton seems to have had a vision of this testimony, seen in the hundreds of Her images from all over the world, when he wrote of the "forest" of

Our Lady's statues in his book *The Queen of Seven Swords* (Sheed & Ward 1933, pg. 33):

One in thy thousand statues we salute thee
On all thy thousand thrones acclaim and claim
Who walk in forest of thy forms and faces
Walk in a forest calling on one name
And, most of all, how this thing may be so
Who know thee not are mystified to know—
That one cries "Here she stands" and one cries "Yonder"
And thou wert home in Heaven long ago.

This great 20th century philosopher, who dazzled the world with his paradoxes, sees that in all the thousands of images and titles of the Queen, we honor just the one person, the one Mother, the one Queen.

Even walking *in a veritable forest of Her images*, we call on one name. Those who do not know Her cannot understand this universal devotion. "Who know thee not *are mystified* to know..."

One says She is at Lourdes, another at Fatima, another here, another there. Some ask why "Our Lady of the Innocents," or why "Our Lady of All Nations," or why any one of hundreds of titles?

But, all the many titles given to Her speak of many victories.

This Is the Time

Chesterton continues (and we have taken the liberty of modifying the last two in summary of the many other lines of this beautiful verse):

In all thy thousand images we salute thee,
Claim and acclaim on all thy thousand thrones
Hewn out of multicolored rocks and risen
Stained with the stored-up sunsets in all tones—
Brought from all nations of the world to
Show the world its Queen and Her appeal,
That to thy Son, O Queen, all the world will kneel.

The Castle of Ourem for over a thousand years was the center of ecclesiastical and civil authority in the area of Fatima. Within its walls, images of Our Lady from all nations of the world have now been assembled, one of which has a recess beneath the heart to receive names of millions from the four quarters of the world.

Our Lady of All Nations, in messages approved as recently as May 31, 1996, speaks of union with the one billion Muslims, the millions of Japanese who will be converted, and ultimately acceptance of the faith by the one billion Chinese still controlled at the turn of the millennium by militant atheists.

The Triumph promised to us in Genesis and repeated by Our Lady at Fatima will be a Triumph of the Sacred Hearts. Ultimately, it will engulf the world. And we have many signs that *this is the time.*

"The Waiting is Over"

Gazing at that statue in the niche of the Fatima Basilica on the night of October 12, 1999, when the sun would soon struggle through the morning mist, a whole flood of thoughts seemed to proclaim in multiple voices: "The *waiting is over.*"

A few hours hence, as the great crowds would begin to arrive for the last anniversary of the Fatima miracle before the new millennium, we would be taking the statue of Our Lady of All Nations over to the Castle, to be ready for the ceremony following the Pontifical Mass at the place where Our Lady promised an Era of Peace for mankind, *and where She performed a Great Miracle,* "so that all may believe" that *God has empowered Her to keep that promise.*

For the ceremonies and Mass of October 13, the presiding prelate was Cardinal Cahal Brendan Casey of Ireland. As the legate of the Pope, he wore a vestment and used a chalice given by the Holy Father for this occasion. At the very time the Cardinal was speaking to the hundreds of thousands *in the square of Fatima,* the Pope was speaking to thousands gathered *in Saint Peter's Square in Rome* recalling this final anniversary of the miracle of Fatima before the year 2000.

It was an ecclesial event, at the end of which it was announced that the two younger children to whom Our Lady of Fatima appeared (Francisco and Jacinta) would be beatified.[4]

Message Still Most Urgent!

Cardinal Casey told the hundreds of thousands in the square of Fatima that the change in Russia, and the freedom of countries of Eastern Europe from domination by militant atheism, was *beyond doubt* to be attributed to the consecration requested by *Our Lady at Fatima.* "However," said His Eminence, "in the wake of atheistic and materialist Communism, there is now a practical atheism and materialism *which can be equally destructive of faith* and the Christian life. The message of Fatima continues to be *most urgent.*"

---

[4] Beatification was announced for April 9, 2000, to take place in Rome. This was later changed to May 13, 2000 at Fatima.

Legate of the Pope, Cardinal Casey, wearing vestment for the occasion given by the Pope, lifts the Blessed Sacrament in blessing of the sick at Fatima, October 13, 1999. In his homily, the Cardinal said the danger to the world from practical atheism may be even greater than the previous danger from militant atheism (promoted by international Communism). He stressed the renewed urgency of the Fatima message.

The listening crowd numbered about three hundred thousand, led by thirty-six Bishops and five hundred priests. Millions attended by TV. As said above, at the same time, the Pope spoke of the anniversary of the miracle of the sun to thousands gathered in Saint Peter's Square in Rome.

After the ceremonies, the Duke of Braganza (who would be king of Portugal if the monarchy were restored) joined us *to go to the Castle for the blessing and the installation of the statue of Our Lady of All Nations.*

It seemed that all had been arranged by Her who stands on the world before the Cross—Coredemptrix, Mediatrix, and Advocate. Standing on the world, *She promises Her Triumph.* She is no longer the hidden maid of Nazareth. She is the "Conqueress in all God's battles." She is the one of whom Saint Alphonsus said: "At the mention of Her name, all Hell trembles."

The message of Our Lady of All Nations was approved May 31, 1996. Our Lady stands on the world before the Cross as Coredemptrix, Mediatrix and Advocate. She has promised Her triumph.

CHAPTER FOUR

"ONCE WAS MARY"

Her power and Her Royalty

The messages of Our Lady of All Nations, from the approved apparitions in Amsterdam and Akita, shed great light on the expected "Great Event" and especially on the Triumph.

A few days before the October 13 ceremony with the statue of Our Lady of all Nations at the Fatima Castle, we had a preliminary meeting to prepare for the event. Those attending were from Portugal, the United States, Germany, and Italy. Two said they would help with the building project but would not attend the October 13 ceremony with the blessing of the statue of Our Lady of All Nations. They said: "We believe only in the message of Fatima."

Another expressed the doubts which many have experienced: "I don't see how the prayer taught by Our Lady of All Nations could be approved because of the phrase: 'May the Lady of All Nations, *who once was Mary,* be our advocate.'"

Two obstacles on the path to Triumph are revealed here. One is doubt even when, after exhaustive study, the Church has pronounced an event to be supernatural. The other is a failure to see Our Lady as Chesterton did:

And, most of all, how this thing may be so
Who know thee not are mystified to know—
That one cries "Here she stands" and one cries "Yonder"
And thou wert home in Heaven long ago.

For example, for years there were many in France who were reluctant to accept Our Lady of Fatima as though She were in competition with Our Lady of Lourdes. *Some view Our Lady as though in competition with Herself.* The "competition" is only over how She is chauvinistically perceived.

Will we have a Triumph acclaiming Our Lady "in all thy thousand images...on all thy thousand thrones ...brought up *from all the nations of the world?*"

Time of Waiting Is Over

The answer is that, for people of good will, *the objections raised are a needed blessing.* They lead to understanding. And understanding precedes the Triumph. And this is the time for understanding.

If there had not been so much opposition to the fifth Marian dogma, which Our Lady said will introduce the Triumph, would there have been so many books and pamphlets *explaining* it? And would there have been so many millions of petitions to Rome requesting it?

"One cries 'here She stands' and one cries 'yonder,' and thou wert home in Heaven long ago."

She comes from Heaven now to call all Her children together. The time of waiting is over.

At the given time, after the dazzling ceremonies at the Cova up at the Castle, the beautiful image of Our Lady of All Nations was blessed in the Chapel of the

Immaculate Conception by the Prior of Ourem. (The title Prior is given to the "pastor" at the Castle, because the Cathedral was served by canons of whom the superior was the prior. Seven sub-parishes are under his jurisdiction.)

In Itself a Sign

Earlier that day, as the statue of Our Lady of Fatima was being borne through the sea of waving handkerchiefs in the Cova of Fatima on this October 13, I thought of the bullet in Her crown which had almost taken the life of the Pope on May 13, 1981.[5]

"O blessed bullet!," I thought, "which focused the attention of the Pope on the message of Fatima, which he now sees as we approach the millennium, 'nearing its fulfillment.'"[6]

Many signs, like the bullet in Our Lady's crown, and those words of the Holy Father, proclaim that Her Triumph is at hand.

Another sign is in the very prayer taught by Our Lady of All Nations which, as mentioned above, gave so many people pause: "May Our Lady of All Nations, *who once was Mary*, be our advocate."

Like the couple who expressed concern about those words, many have had difficulty accepting the Amsterdam apparitions because of those four words, even though the prayer had been duly approved by local ecclesiastical authority and circulated for fifty years.

---

[5] On May 13, 1981, an attempt was made on the Pope's life in St. Peter's Square. The bullet was diverted from vital organs and after the Pope's recovery, he gave it to be placed in Our Lady's crown at Fatima.

[6] In his book *Crossing the Threshold of Hope*, the Pope wrote: "It seems as we approach the millennium that the words of Our Lady of Fatima are nearing their fulfillment."

No More Doubt

Perhaps the reader, like myself, shared in those doubts. Even though Our Lady appeared at Akita in the place of a statue of Our Lady of All Nations, and even though I had translated the first book on Akita into English, I never mentioned the relationship to Our Lady of All Nations because the messages given in Amsterdam had not yet been officially approved. (Only the prayer itself had been approved.)

Then on May 31, 1996, while we were actually in Rome attending an international *Vox Populi* conference, the two Bishops of the diocese of Amsterdam (Haarlem) issued a pastoral letter *formally approving the Amsterdam messages.*

Out of hundreds, perhaps even thousands, of alleged apparitions, only a few ever receive formal approval. The Church is meticulously cautious. The Bishops in this case had taken half a century to decide.

The time for doubting was over. Not only did Our Lady speak those words, but in the face of all the doubts, *She insisted that the words remain.* She said: "*They will understand.*"

Now it was time not to doubt but to understand.

Time To Understand!

What was it Our Lady wanted us to understand? Was it something so very important that we were permitted to struggle for almost fifty years over those four words of the prayer She had asked us to say to hasten the Triumph?

During that meeting at the Fatima Castle, where the doubts were once again expressed, the director of the Queen of the World Center (Carlos Evaristo) said: "Before a man named Charles became king, he might be called Prince *Charlie,* but after coronation, he could not be called *King* Charlie. He would have to be called, 'Your Majesty.'" Isn't this what God wants us to realize about the power and royalty of Our Lady, whom once we thought of simply and only as the "Mary" in the home of Nazareth and to whom He has now entrusted the peace of the world?

It is already a great sign of the Triumph that millions had been saying the prayer, even before the formal approval of the Amsterdam messages. Apparently many had understood.

Statue of Our Lady of All Nations being blessed in the Chapel of the Immaculate Conception at the Fatima Castle, International Center of the Queen of the World, by the Cathedral Prior on October 13, 1999.

We are told that the prayer will prepare for the fifth Marian dogma, and that *the dogma will be the beginning of the Triumph.*

I have already written at length about this in the book *NOW The Woman Shall Conquer.* Now it is time to speak of the rapidly approaching "Great Event," and of the Triumph itself.

Another Miracle?

As I said above, I began to write this in the earliest hours of October 12, 1999. The sun was struggling through and small groups were beginning to move through the half light of early dawn towards the Cova.

I finally knew what to say in these pages for those who are waiting for the Triumph. From 85 years of experience, during most of which I also have been waiting, I would try to describe what the ultimate Triumph may be. I would try to explain the "Great Event" about to happen. What is most important, I would try to explain *the great responsibility it will bring. It will be time for the Big Voice.*

Will there also be another miracle "so that all may believe?" Might it follow the Illumination of Conscience?

In the vigil darkness, as I gazed at the illuminated statue of Our Lady of Fatima on the facade of the Basilica, I decided to speak of a miracle I witnessed with the Dominican priest-sculptor who made that statue—a miracle which says much to those who wait.

CHAPTER FIVE

MIRACLE OF BLOOD

More than a miracle is needed to change the world!

Even as I was writing this book, another was just coming off the press: *God's Final Effort.* I had written it only six months before. Jesus told Saint Margaret Mary, in revealing to her His Sacred Heart, that this was (in the words of the saint): "The final effort of His Love in the last centuries of the world to *withdraw them from the empire of Satan, which He intends to destroy.*"

To Sister Lucia at Fatima, *Jesus compared our failed response to Fatima* to the failed response to *this "final effort" of His Sacred Heart.*

This parallel drawn by Our Lord, in the colloquy with Sister Lucia, leads to a frightening discovery. It also leads to great hope. Both are in the book mentioned above.

With the possible exception of my books *Sign of Her Heart* and *The World's Greatest Secret*, *God's Final Effort* may be the most important. On May 2, 1999, the day that Padre Pio was beatified, I was wondering whether, with all the evil in the world and with so little interest in Fatima, *it might already be too late.* Immediately, the thought came: *"Look at Fatima in the context of history."*

At once, there flooded to my mind how the atom bomb and the miracle of Fatima placed us at the hinge of history, with the threat of nuclear destruction countered by the promise of Triumph.

With those thoughts, and invoking Blessed Padre Pio who seems to have inspired them, *God's Final Effort* was begun on May 2, 1999.

That same day (May 2, 1999), a miracle occurred in Naples which had been expected the day before. It was the liquefaction of the blood of Saint Januarius.

As I gazed at the giant statue of the Immaculate Heart of Mary on the facade of the Basilica of Fatima the night this book was begun, I remembered my last meeting with the sculptor of that statue. It was in Naples on the day of the miracle of Saint Januarius. This priest, who had spent more time with Sister Lucia than perhaps anyone since she entered Carmel (outside of her own community),[7] exclaimed in awe as the solid mass of coagulated blood began to redden and move and bubble with life:

"This is the greatest miracle outside the Eucharist."

---

[7] Because Father Thomas McGlynn was a Dominican priest as well as a master sculptor, he was given permission to see Sister Lucia day after day as he made the statue to be placed on the facade of the Fatima Basilica. He wrote a book which gives the best possible description of Our Lady, although Sister Lucia found it impossible for a sculptor to translate what she described into marble. No matter how the clay model was shaped and reshaped over and over, it never had the heavenly and living reality. Saint Bernadette of Lourdes had the same experience.

Cardinal Michele Giordano holds up vial containing the blood of St. Januarius which did not liquefy as expected on May 1, 1999, but at 11:05 on the morning of Sunday, May 2, when Padre Pio was being beatified in Rome.

Can Miracles Bring the Triumph?

Yet how many people in the world does it affect? Can God bring about the Triumph of Grace by working miracles? Does it not seem that *only those who already believe take note of miracles?* Even many of those who believe in miracles often fail to respond.

Elizabeth Szanto, to whom Our Lady gave the message of Her Flame of Love, asked Our Lady why She did not perform a miracle so that all would believe. Our Lady answered sadly:

"I performed a Great Miracle at Fatima and asked for the devotion of the Five First Saturdays and how many respond?"

Is today's world so far deadened to the supernatural that even miracles may not be able to save it?

That is why the Illumination of Conscience must be the most anticipated event to bring about the Triumph which, as we shall see shortly, is certain to take place.

That Great Event will be *personal*. It will be decisive. The reaction to this particular and *personal* intervention by God, enabling all *to see themselves as God sees them*, may determine whether or not a vast part of the world may, or may not, be purged by a chastisement worse than the Deluge.

We Ignore the Greatest Miracle

The miracle of Saint Januarius, seen even several times, is always meaningful and awesome. In the six hundred years in which records have been kept, the miracle rarely failed to happen "on schedule." The very constancy of the miracle, through all the centuries of change in the world, is itself a marvel. It makes us think of the greater miracle of the Transubstantiation

Reliquary of St. Januarius

of the Blood of Our Lord in the Mass which remains invariable and constant, at the word of any priest since the time of the Last Supper, the night before our redemption, until now.

We worry about our times, almost ignoring the Miracle constantly with us. We act as though God were not a part of our world, a part of our personal lives.

Saint Januarius was the Bishop of Naples at a time when, after two hundred years of persecution, Christianity had been given a great deal of freedom. Then Diocletian became emperor of the Roman empire and launched the bloodiest persecution of all, because it took so many Christians by surprise. They had begun open practice of their religion. Saint Januarius was taken outside the walls of Naples and beheaded on September 19, 305.[8]

As had become a custom, pious followers gathered some of the martyr's blood in a phial, which was then placed with the body. Within fifteen years, pagan Rome changed with the ascent of Constantine to the throne. The body of Saint Januarius, along with the phial of blood, was borne Triumphantly back into the city. Tradition says that on the way, to everyone's amazement, the blood in the phial (which had become a blackened solid) liquefied and bubbled as though alive.

Extant records date from 1349. The same miracle happens on the anniversary of the translation of the body (Saturday before the first Sunday of May) and on September 19th. On those days, when the phial of solidified blood is brought into proximity with the reliquary containing the martyr's head, it changes not only from solid to liquid, but in color, volume, and

---

[8] The year 305 is calculated from historic records of the Diocletian persecution. The days of the month are from tradition which seems confirmed by the fact that on these days (first Saturday of May and September 19), the miracle occurs.

weight.[9] The phenomenon has been examined over and over by experts of religion and science. There is no natural explanation.

This Time Nothing Happened

On May 1, 1999, the triply locked tabernacle holding the blood was opened with the keys held separately by civil and ecclesiastical authorities. As usual, the Cardinal held up the phial while the crowd in the Cathedral pressed forward to see the miracle.

Nothing happened. The blood remained black and solid.[10]

The next day, at the very time Blessed Padre Pio was beatified, the miracle took place. Padre Pio had bled from hands, feet, and side for fifty years as a living crucifix. He had called upon the world to respond to the message of Fatima. He accepted as his spiritual children all who would make the Fatima pledge and keep it. He said he would wait at the gates of Heaven until all his spiritual children had entered.

Even though the "delay" in the liquefaction of the almost eighteen-hundred-year-old blood of a martyr is so very, very extraordinary, *did you know about this before reading it here? Does anyone even mention it?*

The general press, including general television, seems totally oblivious to the supernatural. The sun can seem to fall out of the sky above a hundred thousand witnesses and the world calls it crystals in

---

[9] Dozens of scientific efforts have failed to explain it. Most remarkable is the fact that, when the blood bubbles up and fills the entire phial, the weight increases by 26 grams.

[10] This is one of the several proofs of the miracle. It shows that the liquefaction is not caused by crowds, by heat, by psychic force. Although the blood rarely fails to liquefy on the dates mentioned here, on December 16, when the relic is also exposed, it liquefies sometimes and most times does not, completely independent of any outside cause.

the atmosphere. An unknown light over all Europe in 1938 causes millions to think the world is on fire. It was the "great sign," predicted by Our Lady of Fatima that the second world war is about to begin, and they speak of an aurora borealis.

No Mention of the Greatest Miracle

As we entered the third millennium, various documentaries on television reviewed the amazing century which had just come to an end. They highlighted the great discoveries in radio and television, the revolution in communications with satellites circling above the earth, the trip to the moon challenging the frontiers of space.

They mentioned the wars, with ten million killed in the first world war and many more in the second, ending with the most destructive weapon ever conceived: the atomic bomb. They hailed all the major sports and entertainment figures of the century. They even hailed the "emancipation" of women, not only with the vote but with birth control. Almost every major event and innovation of the century was recalled in word and picture.

But there was no mention of the greatest miracle in history "so that all may believe." There was no mention of the messages from Heaven *which explained all that had been happening in this century of change.*

Sometimes we wonder if God could have done more than He did to draw us from worldliness, to call us like prodigal children to the home of our Father.

Yes, there is something more. He can cause us all, in one moment, to see ourselves as He does.

This will be the climax of what He told Saint Margaret Mary over three hundred years ago—the "final effort of His Love in the last centuries of the world *to withdraw us from the empire of Satan which He intends to destroy.*"

The last vision of Fatima shows Blood flowing from the Head and Heart of Jesus to the Host, and then into a chalice. God the Father and the Holy Spirit appear above the Redeemer from Whose left Hand the words "Graces and Mercy" flow down over the altar like water.

Presenting this vision in 1929, Our Lady said: *"Now is the time."*

CHAPTER SIX

MIRACLE OF FATIMA UNVEILS THE FUTURE

They cried their sins aloud and prayed for mercy

The miracle of Fatima not only confirms the Triumph but, to some extent, reveals it. Beginning in the next chapter, we will look at "the Great Event" which, we presume, will happen within the first twenty-five years of the new millennium. *It will replicate what happened to many at the moment of the miracle of the sun.*

Impossible To Imagine

It is unlikely that the reader, and indeed anyone who was not an actual witness of the miracle, could fully grasp what happened. No matter how much one might hear or read about it, no description does justice to the reality. It is almost impossible to realize *what it was really like*.

I wrote what was considered by many (including the Bishop of Fatima) the classic on the subject,[11] after interviewing dozens of living witnesses. And it was only after several years, in an interview with one particular witness, that I finally began to grasp the magnitude of it. I am sure, even yet, I have never grasped its full meaning.

It seemed as though the very sun itself plummeted from the sky and was about to consume everything on the earth. The fireball was seen within an area of more than thirty miles. Everyone, without exception, *thought it was the end of the world.*

In that moment, many fell to their knees, crying their sins aloud and calling to God for mercy. By contrast, a few felt only awe in the presence of God's Love and Power. Many lives were instantly and permanently changed.

Totally Different

There have been recent reports of solar phenomena which the witnesses believe to have been supernatural, such as a rolling of the sun in the sky, colors, a Host in front of the sun. In two recent books, I spoke of such a phenomenon seen at the dedication of the memorial of the Queen of the World at the Fatima Castle. Perhaps we can get a vague of idea of the greatness of the 1917 miracle of the sun by comparison.

From the testimony of the various witnesses who saw the Fatima Castle phenomenon, it becomes evident that not all saw the same thing. Some saw nothing but an unusual sky. Some saw Our Lady. Most saw what appeared to be the sun change color and

---

[11] *Meet the Witnesses,* published in several languages. Available from the 101 Foundation.

On August 22, 1996, a crowd at Fatima Castle for the blessing of the monument to Queen of the World stare in amazement at a phenomenon in the sky. It was very different from the Great Miracle of the sun of October 13, 1917.

move. All were serious and credible witnesses. I can testify that it was one of the three most unusual experiences in my life.

But we were not terrified. We did not think it was the end of the world. We did not all see the same thing, either because the phenomenon was changing so quickly that *we did not all look at the same aspects of it at the same time,*[12] or because some of what we saw was created in our imagination rather than being objective.

Not so with the miracle of the sun at Fatima.

When we said to various witnesses of the Fatima miracle that it could not have been the sun which they saw fall from the sky, they said invariably: "Well if it was not the sun, it looked and felt like the sun to me."

---

[12] Some witnesses of the 1917 miracle of the sun at Fatima said they did not see it, even though that miracle was an objective phenomenon. Deeper inquiry revealed that these few persons (less than one percent of the witnesses) had been so frightened that they either tried to get away, or were looking anxiously for family members, and were therefore not looking at the sky.

They *felt* it. The heat was overwhelming. In those few minutes, their clothing, heavy with water after standing hours in a drenching rain, was dry. Pools of water, indeed a veritable LAKE of water in the Cova of Fatima, were in those few minutes completely dried.

This was like the miracle on Mount Carmel when, to prove that God was God, Elias called down fire from Heaven. The fire consumed the holocaust on the altar. It also instantly dried water in a trench that the prophet had commanded to be made around it.

Real Fire

At Fatima, everyone experienced the same thing, and within an area of more than thirty miles! *It was an objective event.* Even had it been created in the minds of the some one hundred thousand who witnessed it, because of their unanimous testimony, it would still have been a miracle. But in this instance, it was a phenomenon caused by God (with no natural explanation, as the ecclesiastical commission decided) of a real fireball, like the sun.

Picture of crowd looking at the miracle of the sun at Fatima on October 13, 1917. When the fireball plummeted towards the earth, people thought it was the end of the world. They felt the heat. Many cried for mercy. The fireball receded.

It plummeted towards the earth and seemed about to engulf it. Then it went back into the sky, which had been covered with clouds pouring rain. Through the scattering clouds it climbed until it seemed to disappear into the sun, as though it had been the sun itself which had plunged to earth.

Father Pio Sciatizzi, S.J., who was at once a theologian and scientist, called it "the greatest, most colossal miracle in history."

What first comes to mind more than eighty years later is that *this Great Miracle did not change the world. Only the few believers, who might have taken the message of Fatima seriously even without the miracle, are changing the world.*

Yet, Our Lady said the miracle was *"so that all may believe."*

The Chastisement?

Of all the prophecies Our Lady made at Fatima, only one was difficult to believe. That was the prophecy that Her Immaculate Heart will triumph—that an Era of Peace will be granted *to mankind.*

All the other prophecies, even that "several entire nations will be annihilated" (since there are more than enough atomic weapons on hand to do it), were easy to believe. Most of them have already come true.

But, the miracle itself is a message. It shows us that a fireball could come upon the earth in a moment and wipe out all life in its radius, as easily as the fireball at Fatima dried everything it engulfed.

Would such a "purification" come if men do not respond to the message from Heaven given in the frightening splendor of this miracle?

If so, it offers great hope.

At that moment of the falling sun, when tens of thousands of people thought the world was about to end, most of them cried out to God for mercy. *And the fireball, which seemed about to consume them, dried the water and all their clothing but left them unharmed—and many were spiritually changed.*

Why were some not frightened? Most were terrified. Many were confessing their sins aloud and crying to Heaven for mercy. Parents were throwing themselves protectively over their children. Some tried to run from the fire. Many were just paralyzed with fear. Yet a few just marveled at the wonder and were not afraid.

These few were frequent Communicants. To them, anything from God was good. Anything from the Heavenly Father could not harm them. They were filled with wonder and *they were not afraid.*

The Illumination

Recently, it has been made known that the miracle, while signifying many things, also signifies the intervention of God the Father.[13]

He is a most loving Father Who wishes to draw all the prodigal children of the world into the consuming warmth of His Love. Today, like the prodigal far from the father and eating the husks fed to pigs, mankind will be awakened to its sad plight.

The Illumination of Conscience, like the sun plunging from the sky over those thousands of people at Fatima, *will be to draw the prodigal world back to the Father.*

In the approved revelations of God the Father to Mother Eugenia,[14] the Father said: *"My children*

---

[13] This is treated at length in the monumental work by Dr. Thomas Petrisko in *The Fatima Prophecies*, St. Andrew's Productions, McKees Rock, PA 15136, especially all of Chapter 51.

[14] The commission of ecclesiastical inquiry on the revelations to Mother Eugenia Ravasio was convened in 1935. After ten years, Bishop Alexander Caillot, of Grenoble, France, issued the declaration that they were authentic. However, they have only recently become widely known.

who have lost your faith, raise your eyes. You will see shining rays coming to illuminate you. I am the Shining Sun. I warm you. Look and you will recognize I am your Creator, Father. I am your only and unique God. It is because I love you that I come to make you love Me so you will be saved."

We will be speaking now of this coming "Great Event," the Illumination of Conscience. Hopefully many will have this book before it happens so that, like those few at Fatima, they will be not afraid.

The Ilumination, for many, will be a devastating experience.

Will Tear Their Hair

We don't like to quote the visionaries of Medjugorje before they are formally approved by the Church, even though we may believe in them. But, without anticipating the judgment of the Church, there is one Medjugorje message about the Ilumination that we would like to quote, not as a "revelation," but because it seems to describe how, unfortunately, many people in the world (as in the case of the miracle of Fatima) may react.

In 1985, one of the visionaries reported Our Lady as saying: *"Pray for unbelievers. People will tear their hair. Brothers will plead with brothers. They will curse their past lives lived without God. For many it will be too late. Now is the time for conversion."*

It is to be feared that, for many, the Ilumination may be too late for conversion. Many may be tempted to despair. That is why Father Philip Bebie felt it was urgent to describe in advance the Great Event before it happened.

CHAPTER SEVEN

THE GREAT EVENT

Seeing ourselves as God sees us

Most of what you are about to read in this chapter was completed in Father Bebie's last years of consuming cancer. It was intended to be read AFTER the Great Event, after the Illumination of Conscience had actually been experienced.

For many, this will probably be the case. You are fortunate if you are reading it in advance. You will be prepared.

This is how it will seem:

> A short time ago, abruptly, *all on earth felt the intervening of God. To each one of us, He unveiled the innermost secrets of our heart.* His inexorable light seared our consciences and showed us to ourselves as in a flawless mirror. The truth was vivid in our minds. We saw the awful blight of our sinfulness, the excruciating pain of it, and

knew in an instant what our eternity would be because of it. The Lord's mercy scoured away all pretension. By His merciful intrusion, we knew ourselves—oh, how we knew ourselves, in His light. We felt the Warning.

Like Conversion of Saint Paul

The Warning was like the conversion of Saint Paul the Apostle, who was penetrated by the same light we have recently endured. He was on the Damascus road, journeying to that town to persecute the newly converted Christian Jews who lived there. In a glorious vision it was revealed to him that he was assailing not only the members of the Church, but Jesus Himself, the very Lord of Heaven and earth! The blinding light of the Risen Christ convicted him of sin. Paul heeded the warning Jesus had given him; he repented and became His faithful follower, and left his former life behind.

Has not the same enlightenment been accorded to us all in the Warning? The grace once granted to an individual has finally penetrated every human heart in a single, sudden burst of divine light. We have felt the same grace, the same light, that Paul did. God would have the whole world respond just as Paul did. We must now repent of the sin the Lord has shown us in ourselves by the Warning, and amend our lives, following Jesus.

Made Us Aware

The Warning made us aware of God. Everyone, unbeliever as well as believer, now can declare that God has touched us with His immeasurable power. *He has intervened in an unprecedented manner to make all people aware of His existence, His mercy, His sovereign rulership,* His love for us and His concern for our salvation. There is a God, and He is good. No one can now any longer deny Him unless he chooses to fling the truth back in

God's face. The Warning has made God evident. We have felt His power in our bones.

The Warning shows us our sins. It was predicted as a "correction of the conscience of the world." *The Scriptures foretold long ago that Jesus would send the Holy Spirit to "convict the world of sin."* If we did not fully understand before what that meant, we do now, by the power of the Warning.

Sin (our resistance to becoming the loving kind of person God is) results in many unloving deeds, decisions, and attitudes. These were all vividly clear in the brilliant light God shone in our souls.

Our consciences were thoroughly illuminated at that moment, exposing all the self-deception we are so clever at, pulling out the dead memories that have never been leavened with love, uncovering the lies we told ourselves, the compromises we made.

We saw so blatantly the many harsh, stubborn, and unkind decisions we have made, the times we cruelly trod on the feelings of other people, coveted their possessions, envied their good fortune, and rejoiced at their failures. Then we groaned with anguish when God revealed to us the neglect, the refusal to help, the undone deeds and the unfulfilled plans. We have heard Him say to us, "Why have you persecuted Me?"

Mercifully Brief

The Warning was a taste of eternity. Time stopped for a moment during the Warning, and the truth of timeless existence tumbled in on all of us. It was no longer possible, because of the Warning, to hide from ourselves.

All we ever did was before our eyes, seen all at once, in a single glance. We knew then how God's gaze crosses all barriers and grasps the uttermost secrets. He shared with us, for our conversion, how He sees us, and we beheld, in an instant mercifully brief, whatever in us was displeasing to Him. What we understood was our eternal state, should we have died at that time.

We suffered for a moment the pain of our sin, the pain of separation from God, the pain of purgatory or hell. God let us see it all, in the Warning.

God's Mercy

The Warning was a mercy from God. By the Warning, we became aware that we are not yet what He wants us to be. *We felt the pain of being unlike Him, far from Him.* His will is for us to become like Himself, happy in all that He is, and to become close to Him.

Sin is the only impediment to that. It prevents us from achieving perfect, even eternal happiness.

God unveiled our sinfulness to us in the Warning, not out of revenge, for vengefulness is foreign to His Heart, but rather out of love and mercy. He wants us to never have to suffer again the pain we felt in the Warning. His mercy allowed us to sample the pain that sin bequeaths to us. The Warning was truly a mercy from God.

The Warning is a sign of the future. It is the major turning point in world history, the most important "sign of the times." The Warning tells us that all that has gone before in the entire course of world history now focuses on the years just ahead of us. Our age is absolutely critical for the salvation of the human race. *A large proportion of all the people who have ever lived are actually living on earth right now. They must have the opportunity to hear and know of God's plan of salvation for them.*

They need to learn that Jesus has come to take away their sins. All must understand that sin alone deprives us of happiness and the glory of God. Sin is our only real enemy, the only adversary that can destroy us forever.

The Warning has prepared all the world's people for the message of the Gospel, prepared them all for Jesus and His life. By the Warning, we all know of our sin. We know we need a Saviour. The Warning is the first step for the conversion of the entire world. Without knowing our own sin, we would never understand how much we need Jesus and His forgiveness.

Never Before in History

The Warning is a direct intervention from God. *Never before has God acted directly and universally to make everyone in the world completely aware of their sinfulness before His holiness.* The preaching of the Gospel through the witness of the Church has been available for centuries, so it is not as if He had never made such a revelation of this kind before.

It has not happened in history before that He has acted with such power, such precision, such instancy. *The times must be very special. There must not be much time left for repentance.* As a race, we have repudiated the Gospel message so often and responded to it so sluggishly that what God meant the world to be, in peace, never came to be. The constant pleadings of Mary for us to turn back to God, and Her remonstrances over the years while we listened not, are, for believers, sufficient evidence that the present age is even worse than earlier ones. But time is running out.

"The times" are about to end, and a new age of peace is promised. The Warning is the first dramatic sign to all that the old age is ending. It is not God's wish that we be among those who refused to repent in time. Not in all the ages is it ever His wish that even a single one of His little ones be lost.

He has intervened so that the danger would be manifest, the evil of the present age unmasked, and the darkness of false "enlightenment" be exposed. If the world has not wanted to listen to the truth, and the Father's little ones are being misled, He, in His sovereign majesty and power, will compel it to listen. With the Warning, He sweeps away all the sophistry and deception with which Satan has obscured the light of the Gospel.

Time of Decision

The Warning calls us to choose. We know now, by the grace of the Warning, that each of us has a fateful choice to make. We can choose either to flee from our sin or remain in it. Despite the power of the Warning, we still have our freedom to choose—we possess a free will. If God took that away from us, we would no longer be human, able to love or to refrain from loving. We have the ability to say "Yes" or "No," and the Warning confronts us with that responsibility.

There is no middle ground. The only choice we have is to be for God or against Him. The situation is just as it was on Mount Carmel, when Elijah called God's people to stand with him and the Lord or with the prophets of Baal and Ashteroth. Like them, we have a choice: choose God or no-gods; life or death.

The Warning has made it impossible to delay a decision any longer. To delay is itself a choice for sin. To obtain everlasting life with God, we have to amend our lives as disciples of the Lord Jesus, Who alone knows the Way to the Father. The alternative is to be lost forever in the pain we fleetingly felt when we knew the Warning. Bliss or agony—Heaven or hell—that is the dilemma. Everything for us depends on which path we select for ourselves.

CHAPTER EIGHT

THE TRIUMPH

It is certain. It has begun.

What you are about to read in this chapter, up to the last paragraphs, was written entirely by Father Philip. It reads now like his message from beyond the grave. *He begins by reminding us that the promise of Our Lady of Fatima* (that Her Immaculate Heart will Triumph) *is "unconditional."*

"My Immaculate Heart will Triumph!" *This prophecy of Our Lady of Fatima,* unlike most of the others, *is unconditional*; it will come to pass. Nothing will prevent it from happening. The Triumph is a certainty. To achieve it is the very purpose for which the Mother of God has been visiting and importuning us for so long a time.

"In the end," she assures us, " My Immaculate Heart will Triumph."

At the climax of the battle between good and evil, between the Church (Mary especially) and the Dragon (Satan and his followers), goodness will be totally Triumphant over wickedness. The struggle will be over. The Evil One will be defeated, his head crushed by Her heel. The Woman shall conquer.

Already Taken Place in Her

In Mary's own Heart, good has already triumphed absolutely. There is no sin in Her. She is already glorified in heaven, untouched in any way by evil's contamination. Victory over evil has reached its zenith in Her Immaculate Heart.

The coming of the Triumph of that Heart, however, must signify more than Her own personal Triumph. The prophecy refers to *Her Triumph happening in us*, as sin is cast out through repentance, and love reigns in the world. In the Triumph, our hearts will become like Hers. Her Triumph is *victory over evil in our own hearts*. This is what happens at the moment of our conversion from sin. The Triumph of the Immaculate Heart takes hold when a heart turns toward God with Mary's faith and surrender.

When we say "Yes" to God, declaring our "fiat" as She did, *the Triumph begins in us*. She allowed God to be all in Her. As God's messenger, She invites us to accept the saving power of God calling us to repentance. Our Triumph begins when we say "Yes" to Him, and it grows and puts down roots more deeply until that Day when we will be raised up with Christ, just as Mary was raised up in Her Assumption.

The Triumph will appear on earth, "in the end," *when everyone in the world consents to repeat the "Yes" of Mary* given to God when she consented to become Mother to His Holy One, Jesus.

Already Begun

Therefore, the Triumph has already begun, because many the world over *have already listened* to the Marian messages over the years, and have made the choices She asked. They have said "Yes" to the Lord. They have joined with Mary in prayer and sacrifice to help save us all and bring the Era of Peace.

In some, this Triumph of a faith-filled "Yes" has been in their hearts for many years, even from childhood. The prayers and virtuous lives of these people have certainly brought blessing and protection to an undeserving generation.

For the vast majority, the Triumph seems to have not yet begun. It is to these children of Hers that the Blessed Mother directs Her appeals. She does not want them to be lost. They must and will turn to the Lord and be saved. In them also, the Triumph will come.

By Her prophecy quoted above, the Queen of Heaven assures us that the present situation will be reversed by the intervention of God. By His great mercy, by the intercession of the Immaculate Heart and of those who join with Her in Her efforts to turn the world around, it will happen.

The conversion of the world is sure to come. The world will become His by our conversion and His intervention. The Triumph of the Immaculate Heart will arrive.

Will Glorify Mary

The Triumph will glorify Mary, the Mother of God. God "wishes to establish in the world devotion to the Immaculate Heart." He wills to glorify His Mother on earth. His intention in this regard is obvious when we consider the implications of Her Assumption, a mystery which assures us that *He has already given to Her personally all the glory She can receive.* He fills Her with glory through Jesus, Her Son, Who has that glory as His very own. He Who is "full of grace and of truth," the "Only begotten of the Father" "on Whom His favor rests," wants to glorify His own Mother to the utmost.

We are to support Him in this enterprise. We glorify Mary with Him. We must acknowledge before all men and women the marvelous work He has accomplished in Her, making Her more beautiful than the sun and stars, more comely than the moon, crowning Her Queen of all in the dazzling raiment of the Lord's light.

We will glorify Her by obeying Her perennial summons to repentance, by imitating Her response to Jesus, by proclaiming Her name as Mother of God and Mother of the Church. God wants it to be known the world over that the Triumph of good over evil is meant to come, and certainly will come, through Her Immaculate Heart. She will be glorified by both God and us on earth, for it will become manifest that God has worked the Triumph through Her.

A Conversion Event

The Triumph will be a conversion event that will be so powerful and universal that all will be compelled to praise God for the magnificent works He has done in His creature, Mary. The awesome might that this humble handmaiden possesses as she shares in the redemption of the world will be abundantly clear before all eyes.

The Triumph will be recognizable in the total conversion of the world. *It will be a historical event of such magnitude that it will make all former moments of glory seem like shadows.* God will accord immense glory to Mary, the Immaculate Heart, and *we will then begin to comprehend with what glory He intends to adorn each of us,* in our turn. Mary will show forth, in Her Triumph, the inestimable glory promised to the Church (to each one of us). Our destiny is the same as Hers, if we repent of our sins and seek the Lord with our whole heart. We too will be glorified by God with Jesus and Mary, and with the same glory of the Holy Spirit They have received from the Father.

Higher Calling

There are other meanings and consequences of the Triumph. For some, the conversion experience will lead to a higher calling for which it would be well to prepare. At the moment of the Great Event and especially in the immediate years which follow, *there will be a great need for priests and consecrated souls.*

Father Lamy[15] said the Era of Peace brought about by Our Lady *will result in a period of great holiness* which will take a generation to bring about. He foresaw in this time a great flourishing of religious vocations.

While the Second Vatican Council spoke of the absolute need for active involvement of the laity, at the time of the Ilumination, there will be a desperate need for priestly vocations and of vocations to the religious life which declined in the previous years (as sadly foretold by Our Lady at Akita).

Consider it Now!

If the reader should be one of those who feels a higher calling, now would be the time to consider it.

The Triumph in the world will be Eucharistic. The need for priests will seem impossible to satisfy. The diaconate will flourish.

---

[15] Pere Lamy was likened by his own Bishop, who introduced his cause for beatification, to St. John Vianney. He had visions and made prophecies.

The Three Children of Fatima, two of whom have been declared "Blessed." The eldest, Sister Lucia, became a Carmelite nun. She reminds us of that "higher calling" to the priesthood and to religious life, which should be heard by many in the coming era of triumph.

Existing (one might be tempted to say "surviving") religious communities will have applicants knocking at their doors. They must be ready for the spiritual formation of new members by the example and holiness of their remnant members. Blessed will be those who will not have abandoned monasteries and convents because of too many empty rooms! There will not be enough to meet the need.

If the conversion event should lead the person reading these lines to a higher vocation, it would be well to think even now of what will be greatest need at that moment, and *what seminary or religious community would be the best place to meet that need.*

In these past years, Satan's spiritual warfare has caused many to leave the priesthood and religious life. But from the midst of the carnage, some new communities have emerged. Some older communities have branched back to the purity of their rules. Perhaps one should consider especially seminaries and communities with a deep devotion to Mary and to the Eucharist. Those are the two pillars of Triumph foreseen by Saint John Bosco.

CHAPTER NINE

TO HASTEN THE TRIUMPH

What has been delayed can be hastened!

The Triumph has been delayed. Even in the very beginning of this century, an age of wars and great suffering, Our Lady tried to make it clear that peace would come quickly if people would only heed Her requests: "If people do as I ask, there will be peace;" if not—calamity!

The Triumph could have occurred in 1917, had we listened and heeded. Again, in 1929, she came and asked for the consecration of Russia to Her Immaculate Heart, saying "now is the time." Repeatedly, She has pleaded with us, but because of our lack of response, the Triumph has been delayed.

Can Be Hastened

But if it can be delayed, surely it can be hastened! We must hurry and persuade others to hurry. *The Warning impels us.* Many are in danger of perdition. They are our brothers and sisters. We must help them by doing the most we can to bring about the Triumph of the Immaculate Heart quickly.

Prayer hastens the Triumph. It accelerates the transformation of the heart. Only prayer can bring about the process that produces in the heart the kind of holiness found in the Hearts of Jesus and Mary. Prayer alone opens the heart to the transforming love of the Father.

Even Jesus, the very Son of the Father, equal to Him in all things, had to pray. He prayed so well that His whole human life became a prayer. Because He prayed perfectly, the Holy Spirit formed His Sacred Heart into the glorious Vessel of Divine Life that we know It now to be.

The same Spirit is working in our hearts continually by His grace, according to the degree that we open to Him in prayer.

As we pray, He acts with power and love in our hearts to make them more like the Hearts of Jesus and Mary. The Triumph is hastened in us personally by prayer.

Our Lady Requested Prayer

Our Lady always reminded us of this most fundamental activity when She visited us in Her apparitions. *She never failed to insist on prayer*, calling the visionaries who saw Her to prayer and conveying to us, through them, Her demand that we return to prayer.

There is no other way to reach God.

We are surrounded by the inexpressibly merciful love of the Father. We are immersed in the being of He Who is Love Itself, yet we can somehow still remain entirely unaware of His presence, if we do not pray.

Prayer opens the mind to realities around us that are the source of eternal life and bliss. It acknowledges that we are creatures who can have a profound love-relationship with God when we turn to Him in prayer, and admits our need of His friendship in order to gain happiness.

Power of Prayer

Prayer accepts not only the possibility, but the necessity of God giving us salvation. It surrenders to the truth that we cannot save ourselves. By prayer, we assert that *we are not alone*, and that *we do not want to be alone*. We are responsible to Another Who loves us and Who is our God. To be with God and to let Him be with us is not only the purpose of prayer, but the very point of our existence.

Prayer allows God to act in the world. It is our world because He has given us dominion over it. But He wants us to invite Him, in turn, to be Lord over it, so that His dominion and ours will be shared, as between Father and Son. He will never act in us coercively, but only with complete respect for our freedom, the gift that makes us fully human and most like Him.

If He is to act in our hearts, then we must give Him that freedom by our surrender, in faith, to His reign. The kingdom will come on earth only when we let it in, for the reign of God is a rulership over hearts which are free. Only prayer so liberates our hearts that we can give them over completely to Him and His reign.

Mary—Our Example

Mary understands this well because She experienced it all in Her own Heart, an Immaculate

Heart having no resistance in it to God. She is full of love, given over completely to the reign of God. She is like this not only because God gave Her the grace to become so, but *because She prayed.* She let the Father always do with Her as He willed. "Be it done unto me according to Your word," She told Him.

She knows because it happened to her—God pours His love abundantly into the hearts of those *who open to Him* in prayer. She understands from Her own life that prayer is the answer to all the ills of the world.

So she recommends it to us. She repeatedly commanded at Fatima to pray the Rosary, the childlike, earthy prayer which symbolizes the need we have for littleness. She reveals to Lucy of Fatima that God has endowed the Rosary with special power in modern times; that when we pray with the Rosary, She will hear our prayers. The Rosary is the central item on the prayer program the Blessed Virgin urges upon the world.

"Lost in God"

But it is not the only form of prayer that She recommends. Of the children of Fatima, Francisco was rapidly drawn into deep mystical contemplation during and after the apparitions, and given the task of "consoling God"; Jacinta was almost obsessed with a divine passion to intercede for sinners and for the Holy Father; Lucy remained on earth for a lengthy contemplative-like apostolate of keeping the message of Fatima alive and of spreading devotion to the Immaculate Heart. In the light from Our Lady's Heart, all three children felt "lost in God." It is not so much a special kind of prayer that makes the difference (although Mary does insist on the Rosary). A loving awareness of God is what is most important.

Other Ways to Hasten Triumph

Penance and reparation also hasten the Triumph. The ones who saw the Blessed Virgin were called to special ways of penance and reparation. The sufferings of Saint Catherine Labouré were lifelong, but mostly interior and hidden completely from others. Saint Bernadette went through excruciating agonies of body and mind in the last years of her short life. The children of Fatima suffered not only during the apparitions, but afterwards also. Jacinta and Francisco both embraced self-imposed penances which Our Lady approved, but which were very difficult indeed. Both of these little ones suffered terrible physical pain because of the diseases to which they eventually succumbed, first Francisco, then Jacinta.

Our Lady took them to heaven, which She had promised to do, but not without their first enduring much suffering "for sinners." She had asked them on Her first meeting with them *whether they were willing to accept all the suffering God would send them* for the conversion of sinners and in reparation for sin. All three had answered "Yes." To this Our Lady rejoined, "Then you will have much to suffer, but the grace of God will be your comfort." And so it happened.

When she returned later to announce to them that the First World War would soon end because of their prayers, they knew they had hastened the peace. But it was prayer, penance, and reparation that had turned the tide of evil, not the arms and might of men.

None of the messages given to the visionaries is for themselves alone. They, in their experiences with their Heavenly Visitor, always *in some way represent us*. Some of the suffering they endure is exceptional, to make the point that suffering has meaning and power—power to redeem the world.

We ought to understand this simply by our looking intently at Jesus crucified on the Cross. But we seem to need reminding that the lesson applies to our sufferings as well. We, the members of the Body of Christ Jesus, like the children of Fatima and the others who saw Our Lady, are called into the penance and reparation which can hasten the Triumph and *bring peace to the world.*

Daily duty is penance and reparation. Our Lord told Lucy of Fatima some years after the apparitions that *the penance He now seeks and requires of us is that we embrace the daily duties before us.* He demands nothing unusual. He asks only that we accept fully the discipline that daily duty entails, and the pain it includes.

Such fidelity *will hasten the Triumph,* since it puts into practice what has happened in the heart. We can pray and be converted interiorly, but our conversion must emerge *in the fulfillment of daily duty and in responsible behavior.* Love is not love until it is expressed in a human way. It must be visible in our relationship with others, if it is to become real.

Look no Further!

There is considerable penance in our lives when we apply ourselves to daily duty. We need not look far from the demands of everyday life to discover self-sacrifice and love. *The Will of the Father is hidden in the ordinary responsibilities of each day.*

Not even Jesus Himself performed any special penance that we know of. He simply accomplished His Father's Will, going about doing good. For His efforts, He was crucified, and by His Pain He redeemed the world. So it is with all of us.

The children of Fatima were not asked by the Lady, "Will you please choose the hardest penance you can think of, to make reparation for the sins of the world?", but rather, *"Will you accept the suffering God will send you?"*

Into every person's life, God sends suffering. *The events and circumstances of each day point out to us the path of love God wishes us to follow.* Our acts of penance and reparation are tied up in the little things, seemingly insignificant, that tug on us moment-by-moment, saying to us: "This way to love; that way to love."

The Will of the Father is evident if we are willing to embrace love and the pain it includes. Doing the Father's Will in love is the perfect method to hasten "the Triumph of the Immaculate Heart and the Era of Peace."

Amendment Will Hasten Triumph

Amendment of life will hasten the Triumph. "Men must amend their lives," Our Lady of Fatima declared. "They must stop offending Our Lord, Who is already too much offended." We must give up sin and become imitators of Jesus and Mary if we are to bring about the Triumph sooner.

Amendment of life is the central condition of the world's renewal. Unless we amend and change our lives, no amount of praying or penance will bring the Era of Peace. There will be no peace, no Triumph, until we reform.

Reason for the Warning

The Warning has finally confronted us. Sin threatens us with catastrophe, because sin must be abandoned. We must keep God's commandments and give up our wayward selfish deeds.

Destruction threatens our civilization, our security, our very lives. "Certain nations will be annihilated" if the present situation does not change. Amendment of life is the most determinative element in God's program to save us from disaster. More swiftly than anything else we can do, true repentance will avert The Punishment and hasten the Triumph. We must amend our lives, "for Our Lord is already too much offended."

Consecration Will Hasten Triumph

Consecration to the Immaculate Heart will hasten the Triumph. To amend our lives so radically, however, is like moving a mountain. Surely this is why the Lord wants to establish in the world devotion to the Immaculate Heart of Mary. She proclaimed, "To those who embrace this devotion, I promise salvation." *Devotion to Her Heart will bring us the graces we need to thoroughly amend our lives.*

We need to seriously consider how to embrace this devotion and remain faithful to it. It assures our own victory over the sin within us. Our being devoted to Her Immaculate Heart will hasten the worldwide Triumph over evil which has been prophesied by Our Lady of Fatima.

In the final vision of Fatima, in 1917, Our Lady appeared as Our Lady of Mt. Carmel holding the Brown Scapular of Mt. Carmel out to the world. When Lucia was asked why this apparition of Our Lady of Mt. Carmel with the Scapular, she replied:

"Because She wants everyone to wear it. It is the sign of consecration to Her Immaculate Heart."[16]

---

[16] For further information about the Brown Scapular, we urge the reader to consult the classic books on this subject titled *Sign of Her Heart* and *Her Glorious Title*. Both books are available from the 101 Foundation.

CHAPTER TEN

CONSECRATION TO THE IMMACULATE HEART

The most important decision

In the last chapter, we spoke of how to hasten the Triumph. Before we speak of what is most important in this "ongoing process" (as Sister Lucia called it), we would do well to face up to the specific resistance it is already meeting in the world and also even within the Church.

We spoke at the very beginning of the reluctance of the media to speak of miracles. There is also a reluctance in the Church to speak about the Triumph of the Immaculate Heart of Mary and of the importance of consecration to that same Immaculate Heart, as required in the "private revelation" of Fatima.

Perhaps the Great Event, the Illumination of Conscience, will change this. But, whether then or now, we must understand the role of Mary in the Triumph. Pope John Paul II said in *Crossing the Threshold of Hope:* "I am sure the victory will come through Mary."

We will later give some unfortunate examples of the extent of this problem in the Church, which can be in some measure attributed to a wariness of mystical phenomena. Much of this wariness can be attributed to Saint John of the Cross, often called "the Mystical Doctor," who warned those striving for perfection that visions might even be hindrance to life in pure faith.

The saint was speaking of extraordinary experiences of mystics. He was not speaking of extraordinary Divine interventions of social or ecclesial significance.

Events like Fatima are totally different from *personal* experiences of saints. The message of Fatima, given through three children, was for the entire world. There is need to distinguish between ascetical theology and theology of Divine interventions of social and ecclesial significance.

New Approach Needed

Father Stanley Smolenski, a gifted spiritual writer, points out:

"As brilliant as was Saint Thomas Aquinas, his theology was not adequate for the explanation of the Immaculate Conception. That of Blessed Duns Scotus was used for the papal definition of the Dogma. Likewise it seems we have no adequate theology to explain the added phenomenon of the social consequences in many contemporary approved apparitions.

"It took about fifty-five years (1929-1984) to fulfill the request for the collegial consecration which was required to bring an end to worldwide communism.

"If there had been an updated theology of such apparitions, perhaps there would have been a more rapid response, and thus the sooner would have been fulfilled the benevolent Will of God for our social salvation."[17]

As we said, we shall give some examples of the extent of this need in a future chapter. It is urgent that we face up to the reluctance of many to recognize the important role of Mary in the conversion of the world. "God has entrusted to Her the peace of the world," said Blessed Jacinta. The Triumph rests in Her Hands, in Her Immaculate Heart. This was confirmed by the colossal miracle performed "so that all may believe." Our Lady said:

"Finally *my Immaculate Heart will Triumph*. Russia will be converted and an Era of Peace will be granted to mankind."

Most Important

The ways to hasten the Triumph described in the last chapter are prayer, penance, reparation, and sanctification of daily duty. The key to all is devotion to the Immaculate Heart of Mary.

"Oh, how I love the Immaculate Heart of Mary!," little Jacinta exclaimed. She then added an ardent prayer that all the world might know the power of the love of that Immaculate Heart.

We might add: "Oh, how we love the Rosary which gives joy to Her Immaculate Heart and draws us into its mysteries, the mysteries of Jesus! How we wish all the world *knew* this power and how to make the Rosary come alive for them!"

We have written of this in other books, especially in *Too Late?*, *God's Final Effort*, and *Her Glorious Title*. The Rosary is the first and greatest aid to hasten the Triumph by enabling us to *live* our consecration to

---

[17] From personal communication to the author. Father Smolenski can be contacted at PO Box 205, Enfield, CT 06082.

our Heavenly Mother's Immaculate Heart which is the beginning of the Triumph in us.

Father Bebie says:

> Devotion to the Immaculate Heart can be embraced in a variety of ways, but the one that seems most appropriate today is "consecration."
>
> Our Lady of Fatima asked for the consecration of Russia to Her Immaculate Heart. She promised that this would bring about that country's conversion.
>
> Consecration is immensely powerful, *capable of bringing down graces from heaven that render impossible things possible.* In the light of the prophecy about Russia's conversion through consecration, a multitude of Catholics have chosen to consecrate themselves to Mary's Immaculate Heart, thereby expressing, in the most adequate way they know, their devotion to that Heart.
>
> It would appear that the most complete method to express "devotion" to Her Immaculate Heart, and to live that devotion out in everyday life is by placing ourselves under Her mantle to *belong* to Her as a child to its mother. Those consecrated to Her are decided in their own hearts to be continually devoted to Her and to carry out Her requests. *Consecration is the Triumph of the Immaculate Heart happening in their hearts.*
>
> The consecrated heart is dedicated to becoming like Mary's Immaculate Heart: sinless, full of love. Those who live their consecration witness to the Triumph already realized in them.

They Have Decided

They have *made the choice* to allow themselves to be converted. They follow Jesus without reservation. They invite others to the same wholehearted self-giving to the Lord. Their hearts reflect the goodness and kindness of Mary's Heart. The Immaculate Heart of Mary, the perfect response to Jesus, becomes visible in the lives of those consecrated to that Heart.

For these reasons, all should seriously consider consecrating themselves to the Immaculate Heart personally. Those who have already done so can testify to consecration's quiet transforming power. They sense, because they have commended themselves completely into the protecting arms of their Mother, that *she is continually present to them in a new way*. They know they are receiving graces they would otherwise not have, because their Mother, Mary Immaculate, is looking after them.

They allow Her to be for them what God wants Her to be. They rely on Her acting in them as Mother and Queen. They know Her in a new way because of their consecration, and they understand that being devoted to Her Immaculate Heart will be the assurance of their salvation.

This is a beautiful explanation of the devotion of the Scapular of Mt. Carmel. We hand over our whole being into the mystery of being mothered by Mary. In this, we imitate Jesus, Who, as a little Infant, was Hers, and Who never revoked this gift of Himself to Her. We say "Yes" to Mary as He did. We believe God works powerfully through Her, and that we are surrendering to that power as it comes through Her Heart.

It Is Saying "Yes"

Consecration can be expressed most concisely by affirming that it is the same as saying "Yes" to Mary, the Immaculate Heart, just as She is, and just as God gives Her to us. We accept the gift of Her that Jesus made to us when He said from the Cross to the "beloved disciple," "This is your

Mother." We "take Her into our own," that is, everything we have and are.

We attribute no more to Her, and no less, than God Himself does. Since He made Her His Mother, we acknowledge this. We affirm also that She is our Mother because He gave Her to us when He died on the Cross. She reigns with Him; we let Her reign over us. She is sinless, and we aspire to be sinless too. She is full of love and we want to be like Her. We consecrate ourselves to all these truths about Mary as we consecrate ourselves to Her person. We relate to Her just as God has revealed Her to be, and we hold back from Her none of the glory that God Himself has granted Her.

Consecration opens itself totally to the immeasurable power of God coming through the vessel of the Immaculate Heart. She is one of God's secrets, one that we can never fully comprehend: measureless love and grace reach down to us by means of the littlest one, Mary.

Opens Us Totally To God

The lowliest, the poorest, are always the chosen. The most humble and unpretentious are the ones most likely to be singled out by the Lord to be channels of His might. Consecration to the Immaculate Heart lives in this kind of faith. *It believes that God can do His most powerful works through someone as simple and weak as Mary, the Virgin of Nazareth.* She is not God, but one of us, sharing our human estate and helplessness. Nonetheless, She is filled with God's strength like the stone water jars at Cana, overflowing by God's power with rich wine for the wedding. She pours out this wine of grace for others. She gives it to us to drink through Her love and prayer. She shares in the mediation of Christ.

This should cause us no embarrassment. We members of His Body mediate the same grace of Christ as we baptize, forgive, intercede, love. But in Her, there does not exist the impediment to sharing God's grace which belongs to us because of our sinfulness. In Her case, because She is Immaculate (sinless), *the Spirit of Jesus rushes upon us through Her Heart with such exuberant fullness that there is nothing beyond* the ambit of Her influence.

GOD'S FINAL EFFORT

John M. Haffert

Consecration acknowledges Her universal reign with Christ and welcomes it. The person consecrated to the Immaculate Heart has submitted willingly to God's plan to act through Mary, and revels in the joy of having made that decision. Consecration is an act of humility, by which we bend low as Jesus did when He washed His disciples' feet. It admits its littleness. This admission opens the human heart to miracles of transformation.

It will hasten the reformation of hearts the world over. Consecration assures us of salvation and empowers us to intercede more earnestly and effectively for the salvation of sinners. It is a most necessary ingredient of Our Lady's peace plan, and will hurry its fulfillment.

A Final Effort

Father Bebie has explained above the meaning and importance of consecration to the Immaculate Heart of Mary.

As was pointed out in my book *God's Final Effort*, this is *the called-for response of the moment*.

A statue at the International Center of the Queen of the World at the Fatima Castle is waiting, with a recess in the heart, to receive millions of names. Simply by sending our names to be placed in Our Lady's Heart, we say that *we want to take refuge there*. We say that we want to place ourselves in Her Flame of Love. We say that we want to be part of Her Triumph, the Triumph of Her Heart.

What is more, we can just as easily place the names of our loved ones in Our Lady's Heart. And we can reach out to our neighbors, even to strangers. *We can tell them in these critical times, God has given us the Immaculate Heart of Mary as our refuge.*

After the Ilumination, we can hope most of them will listen.

Statue in the museum/sanctuary of the International Center of the Queen of the World in the Fatima Castle. It has a recess beneath the heart which contains computer disks with a capacity of millions of names.

CHAPTER ELEVEN

THE ERA OF PEACE

The most important condition

It is especially in this last part of what Father Bebie wrote shortly before his death that this priest, who was of unusual holiness and endowed with spiritual gifts, seems prophetic.

He repeats again that *the words of Our Lady* ("If people do as I ask, there will be peace.") *still hold.* There will definitely be peace if we do as She asks— peace first in each person's heart, then throughout the whole of society. It will be the Era of Peace which She said would "finally" arrive.

"If people do as I ask, there will be peace." These words of hope spoken by Our Lady of Fatima preceded a long litany of the misfortunes that She predicted would come upon the world if Her requests were not taken seriously.

It is imperative to realize that Her assertion still holds: there definitely will be peace, if people do as She asks. If, even now, during the "last warnings," we respond with repentance, letting our hearts be cleansed of sin by God's forgiving grace, there will indeed be peace—peace first in each person's heart, then throughout the whole world in society, initiating an Era of Peace, which She prophesied would inevitably arrive.

Had we listened at the beginning, or at any time over the years She was remonstrating with us, we could have averted "wars, famine, persecution of the Church and of the Holy Father." Many good people would have been spared martyrdom; hunger would not have ravaged nations; Russia would never have been able to "spread her errors throughout the world;" the Second World War would never have happened.

But these afflictions did take place. Has peace been lost forever? Will the human race obliterate itself with global nuclear war? Is peace *a dream, an illusion?*

Unconditional Promise

"In the end, My Immaculate Heart will triumph and an era of peace will be given to the world." This promise is unconditional. Peace is coming. It will be the peace that Jesus gives, not that which is given by "the world." People will finally do as She asks, and there will be peace.

It is not an illusion to believe this. The Mother of God has predicted it. Despite human considerations and doubts, failures and sins, wars or punishment, Her prophecy will come true "in the end."

Cannot Measure The Time

The Era of Peace awaits the Triumph. Measuring the time that remains before peace arrives is not possible, since *the coming of peace depends on the Triumph happening in us beforehand.*

We must first hold in our hearts the sinlessness of the Immaculate Heart before peace can come. Repentance must rout sin before any peace can be ours. Love must override every other consideration, reconciling us all in gentleness, before we can see peace come. Families and neighborhoods, towns and cities, countries and nations must be reconciled before there can be peace. Above all, Christians must be brought together again in one Body which is the Church, before peace can descend on us from heaven.

Finally, the peace must be from heaven. Our Lady referred to this by assuring us that peace will "be given" to the world. It will come from God.

Thus the Era of Peace must wait until the Triumph is complete. *Already it has begun* in those who have heard the message of Our Lady and have changed their lives, striving daily to become holy and pleasing to God, seeking to imitate the Immaculate Heart of Mary with their own hearts.

The Warning has already torn untold millions from their sins; in them especially, the Triumph is gaining a foothold. But the Era of Peace will not arrive until the Triumph of the Immaculate Heart is so complete that the hearts of all of us will have already been converted to peace.

A Gift For The Heart

Peace is a gift for the heart, and if a heart is at peace, it can give away peace. Peace in me can make the world around me a more peaceful place for others. By my peace, I am ready to be in friendly relationship with everyone I meet.

Peaceful nations are made up of peaceful persons who have chosen peace as a way of life for themselves. There can be no war between nations full of peaceful men and women. A heart transformed by one's own inner peace can give to the world the peace that the world cannot give itself. It is those who share, through repentance and conversion, the peace of Jesus, Who will inaugurate the Era of Peace promised to us all.

For these reasons, we must wait, we know not how long, for the Era of Peace. It can be hastened by people of peace, delayed by people who reject peace and embrace sin. We only know that it will certainly come, this mysterious "peace." The Immaculate Heart has promised it.

Can Be Soon!

The Era of Peace can arrive very soon. Should the world be rapidly converted by the marvelous events we have begun to experience in the Warning, it is possible for the Era of Peace to come quickly. After all, "nothing is impossible with God."

Perhaps the great wave of intercessory prayer that will well up in the faithful for the conversion of the world will be so effective that The Era of Peace will come without delay. But we have to admit that a longer, even a much longer interval is also possible. Perhaps more likely (given our record of poor response to the messages), it may take many hard years before the Triumph is complete and The Era of Peace begins.

CHAPTER TWELVE

PERSONAL TRIUMPH

Already begun in the hearts of many

Previously, the Triumph was explored as a victory over evil in hearts. *It has already begun in the hearts of many.*

The ultimate Triumph will glorify Our Lady as our Queen, Coredemptrix, Mediatrix, and Advocate who leads us to Jesus, Who sends the Holy Spirit, that all Three bring us like prodigal children home to Our Father. It will be a conversion event.

It has been delayed. But if our failure to respond has delayed it, our response after the Illumination can hasten it. Amendment of life will hasten it. Consecration will hasten it. *It can happen in a short time.*

Whether the Era of Peace will come by Grace or by fire depends on us. Following are the final words of Father Bebie.

The Triumph

World-conversion has happened before in history. Twice before, a "whole world" (as its inhabitants thought it to be) has been converted. The Mediterranean world in the early centuries of the Church's mission was completely turned around by the preaching of the Gospel. Another world, the New World of Central and South America, was evangelized with extreme rapidity when Our Lady of Guadalupe appeared to Juan Diego, a humble Indian newly converted. His testimony about his encounter with the Mother of God, together with the miraculous image She imprinted of Herself on his cloak, led most of God's people in that pagan country into the Church. The conversion of Mexico took only seven years thereafter, as eight million were converted. The whole of South America followed the same course, so that today almost half the baptized Catholics in the world live in that "New World."

About To Break Over The World

A third world-evangelization is about to break upon us. This time it will not be just a segment of the globe's population. The world now separated from God will turn to Him to be saved.

Every nation and each person on earth has been opened to the Gospel by the Warning. The Church is being prepared. The Lord has been readying His Church for the greatest of its missionary efforts—the evangelization of the modern world.

Vatican Council II irrevocably altered the direction of the Catholic Church, summoning us back to our primitive fervor and biblical roots, charting for us a new course which has for its destination the conversion of the entire world.

The Council Fathers speak not only to the Church itself gathered around the successor of Saint Peter, the Pope, but to our "separated brethren" of the other Christian Churches, and also to the world that is neither Catholic nor Christian. The Bishops break the barriers to dialogue by addressing in the Council even those who have never heard the Word of Christ. Their attitude restimulates in us the belief that God's Word still has all the power and life it needs to redeem the masses of humanity. The Bishops of the Council assumed the responsibility, issuing from Christ's command, to preach the Gospel to all the nations on the face of the earth.

For centuries there have been insuperable obstacles, political, economic, cultural, and otherwise, to this enterprise. But today, many of the forces once antithetical to evangelizing are crumbling. Because of modern technological advances, improvements in communications, political cooperation among many nations, multinational resources, and other developments, we are fast moving toward geopolitical unity. *A rapid world evangelization is now possible.*

A similar unity was characteristic of the Roman world in the time of Christ and the apostolic Church. For some three hundred years, the Mediterranean Sea was considered a "Roman Lake" across which missionaries like Saint Paul had free access to all the civilized world they knew, and to all its population centers. The "Pax Romana," or Roman Peace, reigned under the Caesars.

Not without difficulty, but blessed by the world situation, people of the Roman Empire, slave and free, rich or poor, commoner, nobleman, and emperor entered the Church through the preaching of the apostles of the time. God had made ready the world, in the fullness of time, for the mystery and power of the "Good News" of Jesus Christ. With the indomitable strength and guidance of the Holy Spirit, the spread of the Gospel and the Church met with total success.

It Will Happen

Today the Catholic Church looks toward her future with a new awareness of her call to evangelize. Not only did the 1974 Synod of Bishops state their commitment to it, but from the grass-roots, among Catholics particularly, a new zeal to proclaim the Gospel throughout the whole world is becoming evident. God is preparing His Church for the great age of evangelization that is about to appear.

The whole world will be evangelized. Our Lady of Fatima declared that an Era of Peace would be "given to the world." The Triumph of the Immaculate Heart, and the Conversion of the Whole World were all predicted as an unconditional and definite future. All three imply the evangelization of the globe. An Age of Evangelization will begin soon. To us who are His Church, He still commands, *"Go into the whole world and preach the Gospel to every creature"* (Mark 16:15).

We must prepare ourselves for this, the greatest of God's works in history. The Father is going to send us, his little ones, to the four corners of the earth to bring the good news to everyone.

The Warning Compels Us

The Warning prepares the Church. It is the most compelling preparation the Lord could have given us for the coming Age of Evangelization. By the Warning, God demands that we face our sinfulness, always the major obstacle to the spread of the Gospel, and repent. We must be purified.

The Warning also reveals to us that our times are unique, unlike any other times, and that *a new age is dawning for which we must be ready.* There have been "wars and rumors of wars," and we have been tempted to panic, as if the end were at hand. But Jesus tells us, "that is not yet the end" (Matthew 24:6). "This good news of the kingdom will be proclaimed to all the nations. Only after that will the end come" (Matthew 24:16).

Could it be that He was referring to the Age of Evangelization we have been describing? We are told: "When you see the Warning, you will know that we have opened up the end of time." The least we may infer is that a great and final epoch is about to begin: The Era of Peace and the Age of Evangelization.

The Warning is the "sign of the times" which announces to us the "New Times," the period of history when God will act in greater power than ever before *to bring the Gospel,* through His Church, *to every creature.*

All will come to love the Hearts of Jesus and Mary, and love will reign in the world. The Warning was the first of these acts of power. It is preparing us all for the age of glory that is approaching.

The Church will be reunited. Time and again the Bishops attending the Synod on Evangelization in 1974 voiced their conviction in speeches to that august body that unless the Church again becomes one, it is futile to expect the evangelization of the world to develop. Our disunity is an evident scandal and a contradiction to the demands of the Gospel.

Must Be One

The Holy Catholic Church must become one again in order to be recognizable to the nations as the Church that Jesus established. Unity is its distinguishing characteristic. But our common sinfulness has led us astray; history records break after break in the threads that weave together the seamless robe of Christ. Unity, true and full unity, must be attained once more before the evangelization of the world can even be considered likely.

Such unity has to be a gift from the Lord. Pope John Paul II has made assertions along this vein a number of times when referring to the divided condition of today's churches. His conviction that unity must come from God as grace and favor was expressed in his invitation to the leaders of the Christian world to journey to Rome for Pentecost Sunday in 1981 (June 7th) to first pray together to the Holy Spirit for unity, rather than immediately "discuss our differences" (his words).

God is determined to reunite His Church. *The most excruciating pain the members of all the Christian churches felt on the day of the Warning was to see the harm we have all done to one another by not remaining one in heart and mind.*

By now, the whole world would have become Christian, and many saved from perdition in centuries gone by, if we had continued to be faithful to one another. The Warning has made us aware of the enormity of this corporate sin of which all of us are to some degree guilty. *We require a deep renewal of heart in order to reverse this division* and to embrace the full Catholic unity to which the Lord now directs us.

Not only so-called "non-Catholics," but Catholics too, the Lord presses to lay down their cherished prejudices. Our hardness must be melted away for all hearts to flow together into one compact unity.

Role Of Russia

The conversion of Russia is expected to play a major role in the reunion of all Christians. The Consecration of that country to the Immaculate Heart by the Pope in union with all the Bishops of the world was required at Fatima. The promise that Russia would be changed by this action leaves no doubt that it happened:

1) by the intercession of the Immaculate Heart, and;

2) by authority of the Pope and the Bishops. It establishes before all eyes the traditional teaching of the Catholic Church concerning the Pope and Mary.

It may be disconcerting to many that the Pope, the authority of the Church to bind and to loose (through him and the other Bishops), and Mary's power as channel of intercession and grace is hereby shown to be not the problem impeding Christian unity, but rather the solution to the problem. God will set our presuppositions on their heads. Unity will come because God wills it, because He has set out the way it shall be achieved, and because He, not we, is the Giver of Unity.

Mutual Forgiveness

The new Church will be humble. We will come together again in mutual forgiveness. Whatever gifts of the Spirit a particular church has received or rediscovered, it will share gladly with the others. The whole Church will be enriched by us all being together again in one Body.

A fully-empowered Church will become, in each member, evangelizer, apostle, preacher, servant. There will not only be chosen apostles who will go out into the highways and byways to compel them to come in; everyone will realize and carry out the mission given to us all: "Preach the Gospel everywhere!"

It will be an age of conversion unlike any other. The entire Church, gathered together again by its own conversion into unity, will turn outward to bring in the harvest, lying in wait, ripe for reaping.

A Sign To The World

The Church reunited will be the Sign of Evangelization. The Warning will focus our attention on the Great Sign of the Church itself, reunited by the Spirit, from which salvation must come.

It is because we have stifled Her witness by our sins that the Warning became necessary. The visible head of the Church, the Pope, and the Bishops, heads of the Church in their dioceses and eparchies, are, personally, sacramental signs of the unity of the Church who are called by their ministry to protect our oneness.

God wants us to again accept the Church as a credible witness to His Truth, and to this end He will work wonders to persuade us to seek Him with, through, and in His One True Church. It is His way of redeeming us, the "incarnational" way, whereby He gives us to one another so that we will find Him with, through, and in one another.

We must allow ourselves to be taken into that Church and led by it. His Body is the Church, with all the gifts of the Holy Spirit as her patrimony, not excluding the Pope, Church authority and teaching, the Bishops and Priests, Mary, the Holy Eucharist and the other Sacraments, including Confession and indissoluble Matrimony.

Reunited in the fullness of her gifts, the Church will shine like the sun before the nations.

They will see that she alone offers and can give salvation, and they will stream into that heavenly city from all the corners of the earth.

Will Require Time

The Church lives in time, and it will take time for the conversion of the world to take place and for evangelization to be completed. God can pierce time as He did during the Warning, *but the spread of the message* depends ordinarily, even after such a prodigy as the Warning, *on the ministry of the Church in time.*

There has to be, therefore, an Era of Peace, to allow evangelization to unfold. The world will not be brought into the Church overnight, nor without struggle, persecution, hardship and pain. Not everyone will have been so renovated by the Warning that all will immediately embrace the Christian faith.

Local churches will need opportunity to become fully united and mature, strong enough to engage in the work of evangelizing. The process that began in Jerusalem and Antioch over nineteen centuries ago will have to be repeated, this time on a worldwide basis.

A well-developed system of instruction, catechesis, pastoral care and mutual support must first blossom, to render recognizable the Church where all can find salvation. The Church must be properly organized to evangelize the world, and the world may be hesitant to surrender at once to the demands of living the full implications of the mystery of Church. The complete conversion of the world by the Church newly reunited will require much time. We will need the Era of Peace.

The Church Will Be Different

What will the Church of the Era of Peace be like? We may expect an unprecedented organizational shifts in the structure of the Church of the future. Reunion and world evangelization will require enormous alteration of attitudes and methods to accomplish the tasks at hand.

The Church, it appears, will be vastly different from the one we are used to now, and light years away from the Church as it was before the Second Vatican Council.

Act of God's Mercy

It may seem an exaggeration to foresee such a change in the Church and in the entire world as a result of the Illumination of Conscience. Saint Faustina, who lived a life of great purity and holiness, experienced the Ilumination and says:

"What a moment! Who can describe it! I saw the complete condition of my soul as God sees it! I wanted to throw myself immediately into the flames..."

If such was the reaction of a saint who strove daily to fulfill God's Will, what will be the reaction of those who daily deny God?

It will be a terrible moment. But it is necessary to realize that it will be, above all, a moment of *God's Mercy*. He is doing this at the climax of what He described to Saint Margaret Mary as His "final effort to wrest mankind from the reign of Satan." Standing before Saint Faustina with rays streaming from His Heart, Jesus said:

"These rays shield souls from the wrath of My Father... Mankind will not have peace until it turns with trust to My Mercy." (The Diary, 299-300)

Oh, how important for the world is this Great Event which may finally accomplish what all the miracles of recent centuries have not accomplished! Let us do all in our power to make known that it is not a moment for despair, but for hope. It is the moment of God's great Mercy.

Saint Faustina, canonized by the Pope in the Jubilee Year, experienced the Illumination of Conscience and became a saint of the "new and divine" holiness.

CHAPTER THIRTEEN

MAKE IT KNOWN

"Mobilize the laity"

We are told that *the whole world will be converted.* Does that imply a purgation of the world *which would wipe out the unpentant and give the world a new start with a remnant,* as in the days of Noah?

It may seem so at the moment. But there is a big difference between our days and the days of Noah. Christ has come and died on a cross. During the ensuing two thousand years, millions—many of them saints—have prayed as He taught: "Our Father... *Thy kingdom come* on earth as it is in Heaven."

In the days of Noah, the people were eating and drinking, getting married, buying and selling. They knew about Noah and his prophecy of a flood. *But they did not have an Illumination of Conscience.*

How the Word Will Spread

A third world-evangelization has already begun. *After the Illumination, it will be vastly accelerated.* Unity of the Church will be the Sign of the *great* evangelization which must follow.

This eminently involves each of us. And that may be why Providence placed this book in your hands.

From the moment of the Illumination, *we must be ready to reach out far and wide to explain what has happened,* what it means, and what must be the consequences if the world does not respond.

Do you have a computer? Internet? Fax machine? Copier? Many of us have home computers. With e-mail and websites, we can reach thousands! *From our own homes, we can evangelize more people in a day than some missionaries reached in their entire lives.*

A Big Voice will be needed *and each one of us must be part of that voice.* As Pope John Paul II said: *Jesus is saying to each of us, "You, too, go into My vineyard!"*[18] It is no longer the responsibility only of the clergy to evangelize. It is up to us all. *Our Lady of All Nations* was speaking for this moment when She said: "The clergy are too few. *Mobilize the laity!"*

This may be one of the most glorious opportunities in history in which to be alive. It is the moment when *each of us* is called to be instruments of the Triumph of the Sacred Hearts in all the world.

New Means of Communication

Many of us are hardly able to keep up with the explosion of means of communication. One can only speculate what will prove to be the best way for the comparative few, after they know what the Great Event means, to communicate it throughout the world. But

---

[18] The author urgently recommends the book of this same title, available from the 101 Foundation.

we can be sure it will be relatively possible for the very person reading these lines.

We can put the message, even this entire book, on our website. We will even have software for translation into other languages. Those of us who are more knowledgeable may organize others, through the internet, for global evangelization.

Indeed, many things have happened in the fifteen years since we first felt the urgent call to make the Warning known.

One of the most hopeful has been the development of the Eternal Word Television Network. We rejoiced when its foundress, Mother Angelica, was cured of paralysis of her lower limbs. We rejoice to think she may still be in charge when the Warning comes. If not, we should pray most earnestly that whoever succeeds her in the "benevolent dictatorship" at EWTN will be as holy, orthodox, and courageous.

At the same time, Ignatius Press[19] under Father Fessio, S.J., is developing a nationwide network of Catholic radio stations already operating 24 hours a day in most major cities of the U.S.

With or without networks or computers, all of us can offer our prayerful concern for the millions who will experience seeing themselves as God does when there is no one else to help them understand.

Major Concern

Our major concern, especially at the time of the Great Event, is that the evangelization take place. This has been my concern ever since I first learned of the miracle of the sun, the unprecedented miracle for the atomic age "so that all may believe." How sad that there has been no voice in the world, not even that of the Pope, which has been able to get *the world* (not just believers) to listen.

---

[19] PO Box 1339, Ft. Collins, CO 80522, www.ignatius.com.

A Gallup poll in 1974 revealed that, after more than thirty years, *less than three percent of the people of the United States had even heard of Fatima.* Yet more than fifty percent are Catholics or *in some kind of personal contact with Catholics.* It is as though we were afraid to speak, even though we know it is so important.

When will we awaken to our responsibility?

If the general press remains silent on such matters, can we expect that even the Illumination of Conscience will cause newspapers and TV networks of the world to explain the message of Fatima? Who, among all the media's practical atheists, has any idea of what it is and what it means? Who would even understand when we speak of the "Triumph of the Sacred Hearts?"

If the world has ignored "God's final effort" for three hundred years, *what voice will proclaim it* at the propitious moment of the "Great Event," when everyone will be shocked into listening?

Maybe it will be some years into the new millennium before it happens and there may be as many changes in those years as there have been in the past. But a lifetime of experience, and common sense, says: *The laity must become involved. And it must start NOW.*

Experience in Portugal

We have many examples from the past to guide us.

Adelino Da Palma Carlos, who became the first premier of Portugal after the 1974 coup, said that the Communists had infiltrated almost all Portugal's means of communication (newspapers, radio, etc.). When he and others tried to prevent the Communist takeover, they found that they could not get their articles published or their message heard. Typesetters on their own newspapers had been organized and refused to set their messages.

In an interview with UPI (December 5, 1974), the former premier said that, even though the Communists were a small minority, they *"left us without a voice."*

That is what has happened to religion in most of the world. It is without a voice. We who believe seem to be speaking to ourselves.

In this extremity in Portugal, *the people became the voice!* They armed themselves with whatever they had (mostly pitchforks!) to prevent appointees from the Communist government in Lisbon from taking over their towns. Despite promises of the militant atheists to make the poor rich, the people knew the prophecies of Fatima and they saved Portugal.

At the moment of the Great Event, could the people of the world become the big voice to overcome the forces of worldwide practical atheism?

To do so, they would have to know the messages Our Lady has been bringing from Heaven, confirmed with miracles. At the very least, they would (perhaps by internet?) *have access to those messages from Heaven.*

Meaningful Story

I feel compelled here to share a meaningful story about the "big voice," which I told in part in my book *Explosion of the Supernatural.*

There was a foundation based in Milwaukee which disposed ten million dollars a year on various projects. Their principal advisor was Monsignor Hugh Modotti.

One day, Monsignor Modotti asked my advice on how best to spend the money. I told him the Church needed a voice big enough (with enough circulation) to have clout—big enough to make the secular press take notice. He was immediately convinced and said: "I am going directly to Rome and ask the Holy Father." He later told me:

"His Holiness reached out and grasped me by the shoulders and said: 'If such a big voice could be realized, *you would be accomplishing what is greatly needed.*"

For some time, I heard nothing more. Then one day a letter came from the Chancery office in Fresno, California. It stated that Msgr. Modotti had been found dead with his fingers on the fourth decade of the Rosary. On the desk was a letter he had written to me. The letter was enclosed.

The entire letter would fill at least two pages of this book. He had been very busy on the project. Meanwhile, he had to go to Rome for the Synod. Many difficulties had been encountered. He was pressing the matter earnestly because: "Soon the world will have to meet the challenge of God, and we will need the big voice."

Pope Paul VI at Fatima. When Msgr. Modotti asked this Pope whether the best way to use $10 million a year might be to create "the Big Voice," the Pope reached out and placed his two hands on Modotti's shoulders and said: *"You would be accomplishing what is greatly needed."*

Behind the Facts

There is a story behind this which gives it all a very special meaning.

Seven days before his unexpected death, Msgr. Modotti *had offered his life* for the big voice. He wrote:

"Look into the lives of the Saints. After receiving the stigmata, Saint Francis was crying for three years to go to Heaven... Yes, we have to go through a martyrdom of love in our life!

"Mary is the prototype. She is the highest example Jesus left us to imitate... This is the message of the First Saturdays of the month... It is the Cross that counts. We suffer in union with Christ, in union with Mary to renew the world and to sanctify ourselves. In that way, we co-operate with Mary, the Co-Redemptrix of Jesus Christ.

"I am anxiously waiting the day when everything will be consummated... In a different way, I will cooperate then."

The End Of The Letter

Seven days later, he died praying the fourth decade. Was it the decade of Simeon's prophecy: "Your own heart a sword shall pierce?" Was it the decade of the Way of the Cross? Was it the decade of Our Lady's Assumption?[20] The last lines of the letter found on his desk indicated that he knew that his prayer to continue his work from Heaven was about to be answered. He wrote:

"We do what we can. God knows our limitations. We must trust in Him." Then he concluded: "It was a joy *to have known you,* dear John, and to have you as a dear friend. In a union of prayers. Yours affectionately, H. Modotti." Those were the last words he ever wrote.

---

[20] It was evident he had been saying the fourth decade because of the direction of the fingers on the beads.

Our Responsibility

It is interesting that afterwards, the foundation to which he had been the advisor helped to finance the opening of the Eternal Word Television Network. *He was indeed working from Heaven.* This became the biggest single voice in the Church. And, praise and thanks be to God, it keeps getting bigger.

I was not worthy of Msgr. Modotti's affection. I went through a crisis in my own apostolate and I almost forgot. Then twenty-two years later, in April of 1993, I was invited to edit a new magazine sponsored by a group of Philippine Bishops headed by Cardinal Vidal. We named it *VOICE OF THE SACRED HEARTS*.

The day the first issue of the magazine was delivered, I remembered that there was a box of unmarked photographs in the warehouse which I had not investigated for more than twenty years. I was writing a new book (*Her Glorious Title*). I felt an impulse to go look in that box of unmarked, unidentified pictures to see if I could find a picture of Our Lady of Mt. Carmel for the new book.

To my amazement, the box contained a single folder clearly marked "Msgr. Modotti." It contained a 22-year-old photograph which had been sent with the letter from the Fresno Chancellor. It showed Msgr. Modotti in his coffin.[21]

That very day, the first copy of the new magazine, *VOICE OF THE SACRED HEARTS*, arrived. I would be editor until 1996, when the Alliance of the Sacred Hearts would take over. Then in three short years, I would write four books—of which this is the last—emphasizing the need for *the laity throughout the*

---

[21] Msgr. Modotti had been the rector of a Pontifical Theological Seminary and was used by the Holy See for various special missions. He refused to be made a Bishop and even in his last letter wrote, "Don't 'monsignor' me." He founded the Camaldolese Monastery in Big Sur, California.

world to enter the vineyard—to BE the big voice. Msgr. Modotti kept his promise.

May saintly persons like Msgr. Modotti inspire us to *offer even our lives,* if needed, *that the voice of the Sacred Hearts will be heard by a world which seems to be hurtling down the path to self-destruction.*

God has, in His great mercy, given us the Warning. What will we give in return?

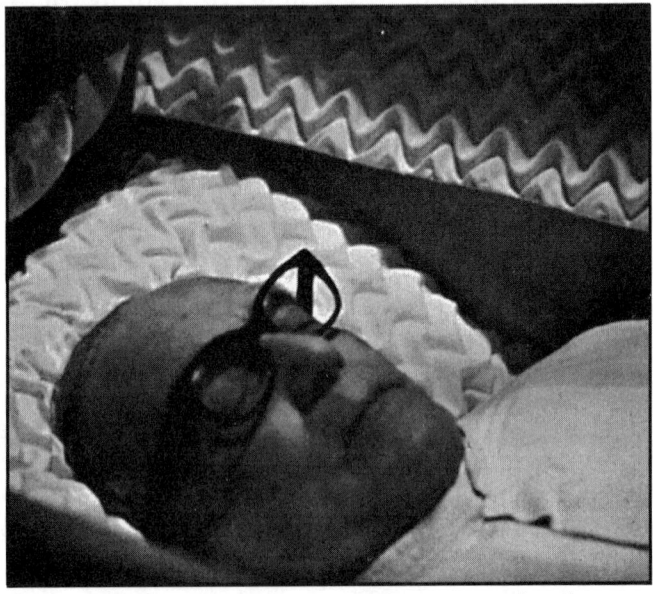

Msgr. Modotti strove for several years to develop a publication which would be a "big voice" for the message of Fatima. A week before he died, he wrote that he would continue to work after his death. This picture of Msgr. Hugh Modotti in his coffin was lost for 22 years in a box of unmarked photos. It was found on the day the first issue of VOICE magazine, edited by the author, was delivered.

CHAPTER FOURTEEN

APPEAL TO PRIESTS

God does not want Her in the background now.

Like Monsignor Modotti, many wonderful priests and prelates in the Church today are willing to make sacrifices, even to offer their lives to give the Catholic leadership our times require. They follow and promote ALL the encyclicals, including *Humane Vitae, Splendor Veritas, Signum Magnum, Ad Caeli Reginam.*

Unfortunately, there are also many who seem to apologize for Catholic principles and Catholic devotion to Mary. There are many who seem to wish that the Big Voice remain a whisper.

The concern of many priests for ecumenism, and reluctance to accept "private" revelations even of social and ecclesial significance, are frequently the reason. Another, which seems odd in view of all the news items and books, is ignorance.

This is a subject we would prefer to gloss over. But since clerical indifference or opposition could be a major obstacle to the Triumph (which profoundly involves devotion to the Sacred Hearts of Jesus and Mary), it deserves even more attention than we have already given.

Events Speak

We had difficulty finding the right words to begin this book. The events of the moment (on October 12, 1999) solved the problem. The events themselves delivered the message. And as we faced even greater difficulty in addressing this question, again events seemed ready to speak for us.

Four Weeks

During the four weeks I was at Fatima writing this book, I was privileged to attend Mass daily at the very spot where Our Lady said: *"I am from Heaven... If people do as I ask many souls will be saved."* And during all those weeks, *not once* did I hear a homily on the Fatima message.

On one of these days, a group from the U.S. had Mass at that sacred spot. I knew the leader of the group and thought: "Today the pilgrims are going to hear Our Lady's important message."

Not only did the homily make no mention of the urgent message given to the world at this very spot but *there was not even a mention of Our Lady's name.* The homily was based on the papal exhortation to migrants! (As far as I know there was not a single migrant in that pilgrimage.)

Of course, not ALL priests who lead pilgrimages to Fatima ignore the miracle and the message. But it happened in this particular period of four weeks. And this fact speaks more eloquently of this particular obstacle to the Triumph than any words might do.

If priests speaking at the very spot where She appeared do not give this message, *what is happening in the parishes of the world?*

By and large, Our Lady's role is held to be secondary, which, of course, is in hierarchical order. But the frequent allusion to the marriage of Cana, where Our Lady said, "Do as He tells you," and then faded into the background, can be misleading.

God does not want Her in the background now.

Striking Contrast

At the beginning of those same four weeks, on October 13, 1999, when the Holy Father participated in the Fatima celebration from Rome, how different it was!

On this last anniversary of the miracle of Fatima before the new millennium, the Pope spoke to tens of thousands in Saint Peter's Square while Cardinal Casey of Ireland spoke, as the personal legate of the Pope, to tens of thousands in the square of Fatima. He said that while there had been a change in Russia, atheism persists and the Fatima message is *"MOST URGENT."*

Is there something the Holy Father knows which most of us do not? MOST urgent *means MOST URGENT.*

We deserve God's chastisement. But in His Mercy, He seems almost to seek to circumvent His Justice by entrusting the peace of the world to "the Mother." He insists that we turn to Her as Co-Redemptrix, Mediatrix, and Advocate to have the Triumph.

A Last Horrible Example

It would seem difficult not to have a single word said about this most urgent message at Fatima itself every day, during daily Mass, for four weeks at the very spot where Our Lady appeared. I wondered whether Our Lady permitted this by exception to make this point here, in these pages.

Then, on the last day (October 15, 1999), there was a large Italian pilgrimage with a Bishop and fourteen priests. I thought: "Finally on this last day there will be illumination of the message which Our Lady, at this holy spot, has brought to our atomic age in the fury of a plunging sun, a would-be consuming fire!"

To my surprise (especially because Italian pilgrimages were usually different), the readings for the Mass of Our Lady of Fatima had been changed. For the first time in all my fifty years of pilgrimages to Fatima, as far as I can remember, the gospel of the Fatima Mass (of "the Woman clothed with the sun") had been changed. It was replaced with the gospel of Jesus being told that His Mother and brethren were outside to see Him and He asked: "Who are My Mother and My brethren?"

The sermon, making no mention whatever of the apparitions or message of Fatima, spoke of Our Lady as "the hidden disciple of Our Lord." The lesson was: "To be a disciple of Mary, you must be a disciple of Jesus."

As mentioned above: What a contrast to the message on October 13, just two days before, from the Pope's legate.

Why?

"To be a disciple of Mary, one must be a disciple of Jesus" is a good message at any time. But here, where Our Lady appeared in all the power of the Woman of the Apocalypse, here where the Pope crowned Her Queen of the World, in this holy place which Pope John Paul II called "The Marian Capital of the World," what about HER message which the Pope has called: *"The alternative to mankind's self-destruction"*?

This is distasteful to write. If this were not an actual thirty-day experience which happened while I was writing this book and wondering how to broach the subject, I would not be giving these extreme examples.

Perhaps the reluctance to speak about Our Lady's messages is tied to a reluctance to speak of *the consequences of ignoring them*—wars, persecution, suffering of the Holy Father, annihilation of several entire nations.

But why do we not echo Her lament that "so many souls are lost *because there is no one to pray and make sacrifice for them?*" Why not one word about Her conditions for the Triumph, pronounced by Her *not only as a messenger of God but as the Mediatrix and Advocate to our atomic age?* We repeat: If this is the case at the place where Our Lady appeared, how little must be said of the Fatima message in the parishes of the world!

And there is a very important reason why we make this exclamation.

What Can We Do About It?

Our Lady of All Nations at Akita, Japan caused a wooden statue to shed tears and blood, and said:

"With the Rosary, pray for the Pope, the Bishops, and the priests. The work of the devil will infiltrate even into the Church in such a way that one will see Cardinals opposing Cardinals, and Bishops against other Bishops. The priests who venerate me will be scorned by their confreres. Churches and altars will be stripped. The Church will be full of those who accept compromises and the demon will press many priests and consecrated souls to leave the service of the Church."

This message was given in 1973, on the anniversary of the miracle of Fatima (October 13), and was approved and made known to the public in 1984, only sixteen years before the third millennium.

At Amsterdam, Our Lady of All Nations said: "The clergy are too few. Mobilize the laity!"

Did Our Lady mean that the priests who promote Her messages are too few? Are those who follow the encyclicals too few? Are those who wholeheartedly follow the Pope too few?

If so, there are a BILLION Catholics in the world. The second Vatican Council spoke of "the priesthood of the laity." One Council document after the other speaks of lay responsibility of evangelization.[22] If we are not hearing the message from our pulpits, let us shout it from our houses! If we are not reading it in the Catholic press, let us work with our fax machines and copiers and/or get on the internet.

When the Great Event takes place we will be ready, if we take our responsibility seriously now. If we are sincere, it is not an option.

A thousand years ago, Saint Bernard said: *"De Maria numquam satis"* (of Mary one can never say enough). And over and over in the ensuing thousand years, those words of the great saint have been confirmed by papal encyclicals, apparitions and miracles, and the testimony of the saints. It has become a part of the Magisterium, especially in the last three hundred years since Saint John Eudes and Saint Louis Grignion de Montfort.

The latest doctor of the Church, Saint Therese of Lisieux, said in the very last words she wrote: "O Mary, if I were the Queen of Heaven and you were Therese, I would want to be Therese so that you could be the Queen of Heaven!"

Two Reasons

Even though it is unpleasant (and in some strange way seems even disloyal) to speak of the failure of many priests to lead the faithful in proclaiming the message of Fatima (even though the Pope said it

---

[22] See the author's book *You, Too! Go Into My Vineyard!*, available from the 101 Foundation.

"*compels* the Church"), we felt it necessary to do so for three reasons:

1) priests, like the laity, need to know so that they, too, will feel compelled;

2) the laity must realize that, if we are to have the Triumph over the evil that ravages the world, they must intervene;

3) both priests and laity must support the priests who follow the Holy Father in proclaiming that the message of Fatima is URGENT. They must support the Holy Father himself, who suffers most. And we must obey the words of Our Lady: "Pray the Rosary for the Pope, for the Bishops, for the priests." *They need our support in word, in deed, and above all, in prayer.*

We need the message of the Sacred Hearts. We need the message of this "final effort" of God's love to wrest us from the reign of Satan. And it is not only up to the priests to deliver the message. It is up to us all.

This book was begun at night as the author gazed through the window at the Fatima Basilica where the floodlighted statue of the Immaculate Heart of Mary stood sharply out of the darkness. The rest of the tower was hidden by curtained scaffolding. On October 17, 1999, the day the book was finished, the scaffolding was being removed. The crown at the top of the tower, *freshly covered with gold leaf,* shone more brightly than the statue of Our Lady in the niche below. It inspired the author to say: *"Hail Holy Queen! Thank you for getting me through this task of affirming your Triumph."*

CHAPTER FIFTEEN

QUEEN WITH PRAYING HANDS

An answer for those who doubt

We mentioned the special prejudice to the message of Fatima encountered in France, to which even Canon René Laurentin's personal experience bears witness. This made progress of the Fatima message in France extremely difficult.

In these circumstances, God raised up Rev. André Richard, a priest of unusual holiness, stature, and ability. He was editor of the prestigious nationally circulated newspaper *L'Homme Nouveau* and a founder of *Pour L'Unité.*

Serious Imprudence

To counter the clerical mindset of resistance to Fatima, and to affirm the urgency of the Fatima message, he wrote *La Reine aux Mains Jointes:* The

Queen with Praying Hands.[23] In it, he said the many apparitions of Our Lady had gained the attention of the world since 1830, culminating in Fatima, but *had gained little attention among theologians.*

"In circles which are believed to be theologically well informed," he wrote, "one often hears that apparitions, even those of Lourdes and Fatima, are purely in the private domain; that one can believe or not; *that they add nothing substantial to the Gospel message, and that it would be just as well not to give them too much importance.*"

Abbé Richard says this reserve on the part of theologians is no longer acceptable in the face of *"the facts,* which have *the growing consent of the entire Christian people, repeated affirmation of the popes, and monuments in the liturgy* (feast days, as is the case with Fatima and Lourdes, with proper Mass and Offices)."

"It seems to us," he said, "that turning away and ignoring the message of Fatima is a serious imprudence. Fatima adds nothing new to Revelation but is a sort of *revivifying of the atmosphere of faith.* It sharpens our attention to what the Gospels teach us."

This is the very explanation given by Pope John Paul II when he said that the message of Fatima "compels the Church."

Saint Grignion More Severe

While Abbé Richard speaks of "serious imprudence," Saint Grignion de Montfort used far stronger words:

"Pride induces us to doubt even what is well authenticated on the plea that it is not to be found in the Bible. This is one of the devil's traps. Heretics of the past, who have denied Tradition, have fallen into

---

[23] Published by La Colombe, 1958, 154 pp. Regretfully, this great work has never been translated into English.

Left to right: Abbé Caillon, Abbé Richard, and the author. It was to Abbé Caillon that the designer of the flag of Europe said he had been inspired by the 12 stars on the Miraculous Medal. This picture was taken June 29, 1992, on the occasion of Abbé Richard's golden jubilee of ordination. The Apostolic Nuncio of France read a letter from the Pope praising him for his great work in promoting the message of Fatima in Europe.

it. And overcritical people today are falling into it, too, without even realizing it. People of this kind refuse to believe what they do not understand or what is not to their liking, simply because of their own spirit of pride and independence."[24]

When Saint Grignion wrote this over three hundred years ago, this spirit of "serious imprudence" and pride was not so common. Today it is widespread. In 1978, a large number of prominent Catholics, including priests and some "eminent" theologians, took out full page advertisements calling for change in the Church. In 1979, Hans Kung, a Swiss theologian of international repute, wrote a scathing report on how badly Pope John Paul II measured up to these demands for change. It filled the better part of an entire page

---

[24] *Secret of the Rosary*, chapter *The Tenth Rose*, pg. 32.

in *The New York Times* (October 19, 1979) in which he wrote of the Pope's first year:

"Instead of setting an example of change, (he has) emphasized anew the disciplinary and dogmatic obstacles—primacy of jurisdiction, infallibility, Marianism, traditionalist marriage ethics...rather than removing them."

Instead of serious imprudence, are we not on the edges of apostasy?

The Good Fruits

Abbé Richard continues:

"At the shrines of Fatima and Lourdes, we see loving crowds gather about the Sacramented Christ in lively faith, as once the good people of Galilee pressed about the Lord. How much the message of Fatima warms hearts with the hope of Her promises! How useful the Heavenly signs which refresh faith! How those drawn to Lourdes and Fatima, gathering to pray openly without regard to human respect, seem to anticipate the coming time when the City of God will unite all, when faith will no longer be in exile! *How much Her message awakens attention and prepares for the great return of Christ,* Who is at the heart of the faith and the principal object of the hope of the Church!"

A New View

Shortly before the council, Rev. Louis Louchet, in his book *Apparitions,* called for a new theological view of apparitions. Referring to the fresh insight of Louchet, Abbé Richard pointed out that Our Lady, who lived on this earth with a physical body now glorified, has a "unique rapport with this physical world." He says:

"The apparitions of Mary, *before being events in the world were first events in the life of Our Lady Herself.*

"If revelation ended with the death of Saint John, the last apostle, the mystery of Jesus and Mary was not finished. Their activity was not restricted by ascension to Heaven.

"One should note with particular attention that Jesus and Mary have a unique rapport with this physical world because they both have the fullness of humanity, being glorified *in body* as well as in soul.

"There is a sort of abyss between souls (even the blessed) separated both from their bodies and this world, as Saint Augustine recognized at the death of his mother, Saint Monica. But Mary, on the contrary, quite naturally intervenes in our corporal world to which She is no stranger. *Since Her role,* by Her spiritual Maternity and Her royalty, *embraces the whole of the Church and even the whole of humanity, it is fitting that She manifest Herself visibly in the world."*

What To Say to Protestants?

It is important that we understand the role of Mary at this time of worldwide enlightenment because God wills it. It is necessary to proclaim it to others.

While we may more easily clarify Marian devotion among Catholics, to Protestants we quote scripture. *The "Yes" of Mary opened the gates of redemption.* That "Yes" *continues its effect at every moment,* to each one of us. This is what we mean when we call Her "Mediatrix" and "Advocate." *We enjoy the eternal "Yes" of the new Eve,* our true Mother in supernatural life. She brings us our Way, our Truth, our Life.

Marian devotion contradicts the three postulates of the Protestant reform. *The more Mary is understood, the more is understood the mystery of Jesus as God-Man.* And if we ask good people we know to pray for us, how can one feel any objection to ask the Mother of our Savior to do so?

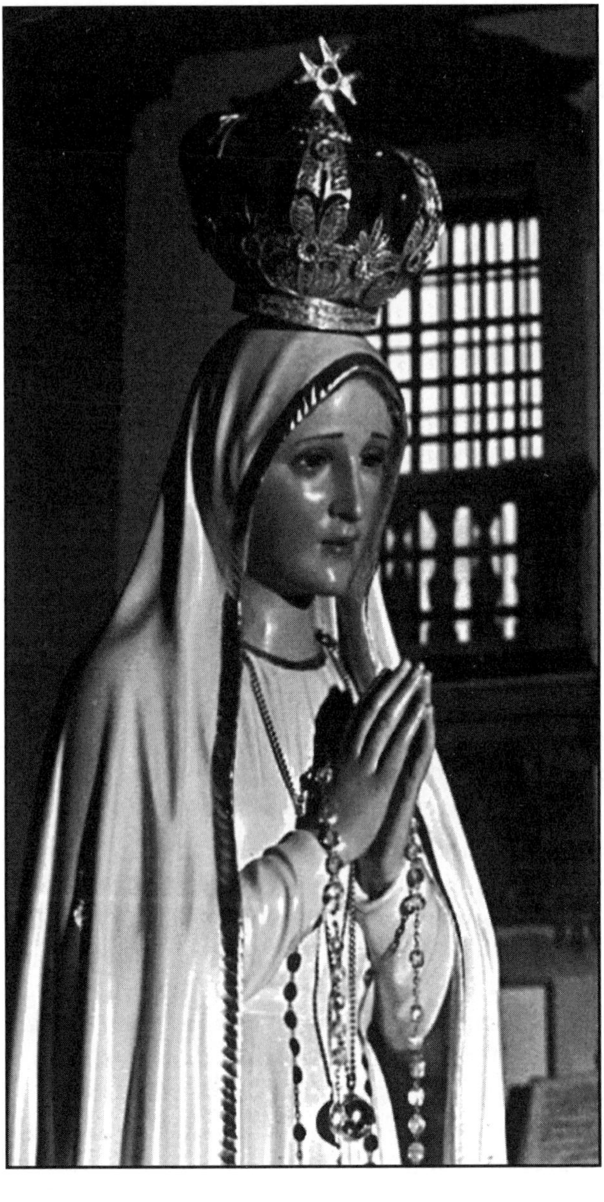

Ask the Holy Spirit!

The Great Event will open doors. The Holy Spirit will inspire us when we will bear the grave responsibility to share what we know. We will have to be the Big Voice—the Voice for the Conqueress in all God's battles to whom God has entrusted the peace of the world in the atomic age.

"Without doubt," said Pope Pius XII in *Ad Caeli Reginam*, "the Blessed Virgin surpasses in dignity all creation and, has over all, *after Her Son,* primacy. If Mary is thus Queen of the World because She is the Mother of Jesus...it is because the Incarnation is a unique event... *Knowledge of Mary illuminates our knowledge of the Incarnate Word.*"

Abbé Richard concludes: "Because the humble Virgin said 'Yes' to God, Her Creator, She triumphs in the blessedness of God Himself and participates in His royalty. Thus the Immaculate Conception, the Assumption, and the Royalty of Mary are as a triple battering ram against which Satan rages in vain."

Since May 31, 1996, we now know that when that battering ram against Satan, the Virgin Mother of God, is strengthened with the titles of Co-Redemptrix, Mediatrix and Advocate, Satan will be defeated.[25] Her ultimate Fatima promise will be a reality: *"My Immaculate Heart will Triumph...an Era of Peace will be granted to mankind."*

---

[25] About the time Abbé Richard wrote this in 1958, his friend Raol Auclair, who also wrote for *L'Homme Nouveau,* wrote one of the first major books about the Amsterdam apparitions of Our Lady of All Nations in which this prophecy was made. Even though many believed in the apparitions then, the messages were not formally approved until 1996.

CHAPTER SIXTEEN

HELP FROM HEAVEN

"I will cooperate then in a different way."

It is a joy to speak of wonderful priests and Bishops who have been the blessing of the Fatima Apostolate. Most of the Bishops and priests I came to know in more than fifty years of apostolate have been wonderful. I speak of several in my books *The Brother and I, Dear Bishop,* and *The Day I Didn't Die.*

I had just launched a new publishing house (AMI Press) and had just published the first issue of *SOUL* Magazine in 1950 when the Bishop of Trenton, who had given permission, suddenly died. He had been my Bishop for only a year.

The Council was about to open windows. Unusual winds were blowing. It did not seem the time for speaking about children seeing a vision of Hell or prophesying that "several entire nations will be annihilated" if people didn't pray the Rosary.

What would the new Bishop do about this new publication promoting the message of Fatima and a brand new movement called the Blue Army?

Whatever he said would be taken as the Will of God. If the new Bishop said even that he *"preferred"* that this publication not continue, it would have stopped. End of story. (This had happened to me once before.)

My Bishop

The diocese (then eighth largest in the United States) was taken over by Bishop George W. Ahr who formerly had been rector of a major seminary. He had a reputation of strictness.

What he *did* about this "Fatima" magazine and movement is described in my book *Dear Bishop*.

During the following thirty years a bond of confidence developed between us which became like a solid rock. When the spiritual warfare became almost unbearable, when it seemed more than once that the apostolate would founder, the Bishop was another *Petrus*.

If secular history does not give Bishop Ahr a niche, I am sure we will be amazed to see the one he has in Heaven, not because of extraordinary accomplishments but because of extraordinary fidelity to his duty as he saw it. Despite a veritable tidal wave of false rumors leveled against us, despite virulent attacks by militant atheism which struck against us all over the world,[26] despite an attempt by one of the most powerful unions in America to organize our national office, he stood unflinching.

---

[26] We were established in over 100 countries with our international center at Fatima, and the official publication in Russia, *Science and Religion,* said the reason for the failure of atheistic Communism to take over the world was Hitler, the Cold War, and the Apostolate of Fatima (the Blue Army).

With one of the biggest dioceses to run, he did not need the burden we drew down upon him. He knew he had only to speak a word to free himself of it.

But he stood firm, even when we were ready to give up.

Close to Us Now

The Church today is blessed with many similar shepherds. The last thirty years of the 20th century were especially blessed with the supreme shepherd, Pope John Paul II, who said "Fatima compels the Church."

And many wonderful apostles who have gone before us are working for the Triumph even more now that they are in Heaven. In one of my books I tell the extraordinary story of the death of the second Bishop of Fatima, with whom I had worked intimately for many years. I was flying to his funeral and a voice said: "There is a message for you in the book under the seat."

It was a book of about five hundred pages. I opened it at random *near the end* and read: "I will be closer to you when I am in the Divine Light."

Another Picture

Was it naive to take as a personal "sign," the day the first issue of VOICE magazine was delivered, to find the 22 year old picture of Msgr. Modotti in his coffin (found on an impulse in a box of unlabeled pictures) to remind me of the promise he made the week before he died: "...when all will be consummated, I will be with you... I will cooperate then in a different way..."?

In any event, that picture seemed to say: "Hello, John! I am keeping my promise!"

Even now, I seem to hear those words as, rushing in my 85th year against the time clock of life, I am writing this book.

Another Sign?

That very same day (May 11, 1993) when the first issue of VOICE was delivered and Msgr. Modotti's picture so unexpectedly turned up, *Bishop Ahr died.*

Once again a photograph became a striking sign.

My wife and I were among the hundreds who went to the funeral. Due to a traffic delay, by the time we arrived, the Cathedral was almost full. Two hundred priests and seventeen Bishops were positioning for the Mass up at the altar where "my Bishop" was in his coffin. Without hesitation, we walked up the aisle of the crowded Cathedral to say goodbye.

He was so lifelike. *I wished I could have had a final picture of him.*

The next day, the major daily newspaper of the city of Trenton (capital of the State of New Jersey) was filled with the story of the funeral. On the front page was a single picture.

It was myself and my wife standing by the coffin.[27]

As I gazed at that picture on the front page of the State Capital's daily paper, Bishop Ahr seemed to be saying, like Msgr. Modotti: "When all is consummated I will be with you. I will cooperate then in a different way..."

The Blue Army, to which I had dedicated my life, was at that moment under different direction and was in a state of major decline. But I felt reassured that the work of a lifetime built on the rock of obedience to my Bishop would stand. (Indeed, I would live to see its international constitution approved by Rome six years later.)

---

[27] I was completely unknown to the photographer or the editor. Chris Edwards, the staff photographer, said: "We chose it because, more than all the other pictures of the funeral, it was the one which seemed to say 'goodbye'."

"You Will Remember"

As I gaze at that picture, I most vividly remember the day I was in a car with the Bishop and he asked what progress I was making in writing the story of the Blue Army. Two years had passed since he had asked me to do it and I had not begun. I apologized saying: "I have difficulty remembering."

"You will remember one thing," he answered, *"and that will remind you of another."*

That is how this book started.

May he and Msgr. Modotti, and all the wonderful priests and Bishops of the past who did their duty in leading the flock in the path of the Sacred Hearts, and who now share more fully *in the advocacy power of the Queen of the Universe,* be with us as we face the future with confidence in Her words: "Finally my Immaculate Heart will Triumph."

The author had been debating taking a camera to the Cathedral but finally decided it would not be fitting. The next day, on the front page of the State Capital's daily paper, this picture appeared showing the author and his wife beside the coffin of Bishop Ahr, his Bishop of 33 years. He felt that the Bishop was not saying goodbye but, like Msgr. Modotti, "When all is consummated, I will be with you."

CHAPTER SEVENTEEN

TRIUMPH NOW

So many changes from 1985 to 2000!

As we have said before, events are moving swiftly. Much of what you have read above about the "Great Event" was written fifteen years before 2000.

Much changed in just those fifteen years.

On May 13th, 1981, Father Bebie was in my office when I received a shocking telephone call. The Pope had just been shot.

"But he is the Pope who will make the collegial consecration!" Father Bebie exclaimed.

He was right. This was the Pope who would make the consecration.

The very next year, after three months on the brink of death, and after studying the message of Fatima during those long days in a hospital bed, the Pope sent letters to all the Bishops of the world to inform them that he would go to Fatima to make the consecration.

To each Bishop he sent a full copy of the Acts of Consecration of the World to the Immaculate Heart, and of the Consecration of Russia to the same Immaculate Heart. Both had been made previously (in 1942 and 1954 respectively) by Pope Pius XII. *He told the Bishops these consecrations would now be renewed by the entire Church.*

There was not time, and perhaps not adequate preparation, for the Bishops of the world to respond. So the Pope sent a second letter the following year announcing that he asked all the Bishops of the world to join him in the renewing of these acts of consecration on March 24, 1984.

Within eight months of the consecration came the first clear signs of a totally unexpected change in Russia. On the Feast of Our Lady's Queenship in 1990, the Soviet Union was dissolved.

That is not all that changed in those short years.

Shortly after the collegial consecration, after two commissions of investigations and repeated trips to

Pope John Paul II had the original statue of Our Lady of Fatima brought to Rome when he renewed the consecration of all nations to the Immaculate Heart of Mary together with all the Bishops of the world. Cardinal Cahal Brendan Casey, speaking as legate of the Pope at Fatima on October 13, 1999, mentioned this consecration as a turning point in history.

Rome for advice, the Bishop of Akita, in Japan, declared that the revelations of Our Lady of All Nations in his diocese were authentic. In those messages, Our Lady spoke of a chastisement "worse than the Deluge," if men continued to ignore God. *The "final effort" to wrest mankind from the domination of Satan by merciful love was coming to an end.*

Other Developments Since 1985

The reader can probably think of many other signs of acceleration of the time to the Triumph. The collegial consecration (finally made after a delay of over 80 years!) stands out above all. It was followed almost at once by the dissolution of the Soviet Union.

Then, greatly emphasizing the urgency of response, came the message of Akita. (It was promulgated in an Episcopal letter shortly after the collegial consecration in 1984.)

Other more recent events indicate that we are on the "fast track" to the Triumph. Five cry out with special urgency:

1) On May 31, 1996, the messages of *Our Lady of All Nations* were approved. They summarize volumes of what the Queen of the World has been saying in approved apparitions for more than two hundred years. They give a specific sign as to when the Triumph will begin. *They call for mobilization of the laity* to make it happen. (Please read *NOW The Woman Shall Conquer* available from the 101 Foundation.)

2) The Cardinal Prefect of the Congregation for the Doctrine of the Faith affirmed that *the message of Akita reveals the third secret of Fatima.* In this message, Our Lady of All Nations tells us that *so far,* She has been able *to hold back the chastisement.* But *if* it must come (if the world does not respond positively after the Illumination of Conscience), "it will be worse than the Deluge." (Please read *The Meaning of Akita* available from the 101 Foundation.)

3) The beatification of Sister Faustina in 1993 resulted in widespread acceptance of the message of Divine Mercy. Our Lady had said at Akita: "So far, I have been able to hold back the Chastisement by offering to the Father the Passion of My Son..." Inspired by God's message to Saint Faustina, tens of thousands join Our Lady in this by recitation of the Chaplet of Divine Mercy daily at 3:00 p.m. (In a vision, Saint Faustina saw the arm of the angel of wrath held back by the recitation of the chaplet, which is an offering of the Passion of Jesus to the Father "for my sins and the sins of the entire world.")

4) *The messages of God the Father* to Mother Eugenia, which had long been approved, *suddenly came to light,* especially in 1999, the year of God the Father.[28] In his monumental book, *The Prophecies of Fatima,* Dr. Petrisko relates these ultimate messages of God the Father to Fatima's miracle of the sun.[29] The Father said: "This is the time of graces, foreseen and awaited since the beginning of time. I come as the most tender and loving of Fathers. I stoop down, forgetful of Myself, to raise you up to Me..."

5) The revelations of Luisa Picaretta were released. They describe the coming Triumph as an era of living in the Divine Will,[30] a fulfillment of the prayer said

---

[28] Published with imprimatur of the Vicar General of Vatican City in 1989, with first English publication in March, 1996. It is now obtainable from many sources under the title: *The Father Speaks to His Children.*

[29] St. Andrew's Publications, McKees Rock, PA 15136.

[30] Luisa Picaretta lived for sixty years solely on the Eucharist. So great a miracle is in itself authentication of her message. Her cause for beatification has been entered. One of her spiritual directors, who authorized much of her writings, has been beatified. However her writings are difficult both in content and in language. An Italian language expert told the author that translations of Luisa Picaretta's writings are extremely difficult. For this reason, the early English versions caused problems.

for two thousand years: *"Thy Will be done on earth as it is in Heaven."*

Happening So Fast

In addition to interventions which are obviously from God, there is another sign of hope: *The development of almost instant communications.*

Who would have thought that a semi-cloistered nun in Alabama would develop a Catholic television network reaching around the world which courageously affirms all that we have been saying in these pages? Who would have thought, even a few years before the new millennium, that millions would have means in their own homes of communicating to other millions all over the world by e-mail?

Father Bebie did not live those fifteen years before the new millennium to see these very rapid developments. But apparently he had a premonition. He had apparently been told by Our Lord that Pope John Paul II would make the collegial consecration. Even when the Pope was shot, he was unshaken in this conviction.

And that is a final sign—a sign that God gives *directly to our hearts*. It is a perception that the struggle between good and evil has taken a turn. It is a perception that the power of Satan has been curtailed.

When devout souls meet these days, they find others thinking as they do—that we are reaching a *dénouement,* a climax of some sort to the long struggle between good and evil.

Really Happening!

In my eighty-fifth year as I write this, I am a battle-scarred veteran of spiritual warfare. I have been at the crux of the struggle between the Woman and the Dragon in the World Apostolate of Fatima for more than half a century.

I can *feel* a difference now.

In spiritual meetings, there is less contention. There is a greater openness to the supernatural. Divisions are beginning to heal. *The prayer to God the Father, taught to Mother Eugenia, is like the parting of a great veil between this world and His.*[31]

It is really happening. *The Triumph has begun.*

As you read this, if the "Great Event" has not already taken place, prepare for it!

Let the Triumph begin with each one of us, now.

---

[31] For an explanation of this prayer see appendix to the author's book *Too Late?*, available from the 101 Foundation.

CHAPTER EIGHTEEN

WHAT WILL THE TRIUMPH BE?

"A new springtime of Christianity"
–Pope John Paul II

What we have written in these previous pages is not based primarily on speculation or private revelations. It is based on sound doctrine and the Magisterium.

In his recent book (published in 1999) on future events based solely on scripture and the teaching of the Church, Father Joseph Iannuzzi, OSJ,[32] concludes:

"As our Holy Father has so often quoted, the third millennium will be marked by 'a new springtime in Christianity,' will be 'intensely Eucharistic,' will at its dawn 'make Christ the heart of the world,' and will

---

[32] *The Triumph of God's Kingdom in the Millennium and End Times*, St. John the Evangelist Press, 1999, 170 pp.

have as its 'goal and fulfillment...the life of each Christian and the whole Church in the Triune God' (*Tertio Millennio Adveniente*)."

Dr. Thomas Petrisko called Father Iannuzzi's book, "the most authoritative ever written on the subject, with historic implications for the Church and for every person on the earth." And in it we find confirmation of almost all that we have been saying.

"The truth will eventually manifest itself," he says, "even if, as in the days of Noah, only *after* the flood arrives."

Already Revealed in Scripture and Tradition

Jesus told Luisa Picaretta that the three great periods of time were 2,000 years from Creation to Flood, 2,000 years from Flood to Redemption, and 2,000 years to the Era of Peace (the era which will be "intensely Eucharistic"). And Father Iannuzzi found confirmation in *The Divine Institutes*: "At the end of the six thousandth year, all wickedness must be abolished from the earth, and righteousness reign for a thousand years."[33]

In 1997, Pope John Paul II quoted Blessed Hannibal Di Francia (confessor of Luisa Picaretta, who approved many of her writings for publication):

"He (Blessed Hannibal) saw the means God Himself had provided to bring about that 'new and divine' holiness with which the Holy Spirit wishes to enrich Christians at the dawn of the third millennium in order to make Christ the heart of the world."[34]

Mother Angelica's Second Prophecy

We have barely hinted at what this Triumph will be. We have been concerned about the Great Event which will herald it. How the world reacts to that

---

[33] The Divine Institutes, Lactantius, *Anti-Nicene Fathers*. cf. Iannuzzi, pg. 119.
[34] Osservatore Romano, July 9, 1997.

event will determine whether we will enter the era of Triumph with or without a worldwide purification of fire.

But *we can say with assurance:* "Let the Triumph begin now!," *because we know WHAT that Triumph will be.*

We began this book with the first part of the answer given by Mother Angelica of EWTN after her cure: She foresaw the Illumination of Conscience. We close now with the second part of her answer. She said: "People will enter Catholic Churches and KNOW that Jesus is there." As it was when He walked among His people 2000 years ago, *power will go out from Him.*

Triumph Will Be Eucharistic

We had an image of this prophecy in the very first apparition of Fatima. Our Lady asked the children if they would say "yes" to whatever God would ask of them, just as we will be asked at the moment of the Illumination of Conscience.

When the children said "yes," Our Lady opened Her hands and rays of light streamed from Her Heart upon the children, causing them to "feel lost in God." And in that light from Mary's Heart, all three cried out together:

"O Most Holy Trinity, I adore Thee! My God, My God, I love Thee in the Most Blessed Sacrament!"

In his little book on *The Real Presence,* Father Robert DeGrandis, SSJ relates that one day, in a house of prayer on the island of Granada in the West Indies, a nun came and said to him:

"Father, I cannot feel the power coming out of the Tabernacle."

She was so insistent that, even though he had never in his life felt any "power" coming from a Tabernacle, he went to investigate.

"I found," he writes, "water had gotten into the container of the consecrated Hosts. They had been dissolved." *Jesus was no longer there.*[35]

We will KNOW

Many of our separated brethren have the light to know that Jesus is coming to be in our midst. After the Illumination, with joy, *they will discover, that He is already here!* We will all *know* Him in a new and most powerful manner.

If Jesus were to return today as He was in Palestine before the institution of the Eucharist, how many of us would be able to see Him *in Person*? How many would be able to speak to Him in Person? How many would be able to touch Him?

He loves us so much that He wants to be present to EACH of us, wholely and completely. And in the time of the Triumph, we will *know* that He does this through the greatest of all miracles: the Eucharist. His reign will begin in the hearts of each of us.

As Father Iannuzzi has shown from the teaching of the Church of the past two thousand years, *in this time now arriving,* "God will rest in the hearts of all the earth's inhabitants who in turn will carry Him in their hearts like living Hosts."

Let it begin now with those who *already* understand what the Sacred Heart described to Saint Margaret Mary as *"God's final effort to wrest mankind from the reign of Satan."*

Lived Solely on the Eucharist

Is it not most extraordinary that two lay persons chosen to foster devotion to the Immaculate Heart of Mary lived for years solely on the Blessed Sacrament?

---

[35] *The Real Presence of Jesus in the Holy Eucharist,* 1998, H.O.M. Books, Lowell, MA 01850.

This is in itself a miracle so extraordinary that Rome demanded proof when the Archbishop of Braga notified the Holy See that Alexandrina da Costa, living solely on the Eucharist, had a message from Our Lord that He wanted the world consecrated to the Immaculate Heart of His Mother.

The Archbishop arranged that Alexandrina be confined in a hospital with constant supervision, beyond the normal time that she might have died of starvation. She received absolutely nothing, not even water, other than a tiny white Host once each day.

That Host was Jesus, Who said: "This is My Body... He who eats My Body...shall have life everlasting."

Alexandrina lived solely on the Eucharist for *thirteen years.*

Another laywoman in Belgium, Bertha Petit, also lived solely on the Eucharist. Like Alexandrina, she had a message about the Immaculate Heart of Mary. Jesus said He wanted devotion to the Immaculate Heart of His Mother established in the world.

He referred to His Mother's Heart as *the Sorrowful and Immaculate Heart.* He said that God made Her Heart Immaculate, but She earned the title "Sorrowful" at the foot of the Cross where She shared in the act of Redemption with Him.

Time of Spiritual Awareness

Why do the saints insist that the Eucharistic Triumph will come through the Immaculate Heart of Mary? Why does God insist on the consecration to the Immaculate Heart of Mary? Read again the words spoken by Our Lord to Saint John Eudes:

"I have given you this admirable Heart of My dear Mother to be one with yours, so that you might have a heart worthy of Mine."

Our Lady said at Fatima: "God wishes to establish in the world devotion to my Immaculate Heart." That is because *through this Immaculate Heart, God will now establish in the world the reign of Jesus in the Eucharist.*

As we said above, we had a preview of this Triumph when, *in the light from Her Heart,* the children of Fatima "felt lost in God" and exclaimed with one voice: *"O Most Holy Trinity, I adore Thee! My God, My God, I love Thee in the Most Blessed Sacrament!"*

At that moment the three little children were intensely AWARE of GOD. This will happen to us at the moment of the Great Event.

Our recent book, *God's Final Effort,* speaks at length of this awareness. We do not have to wait for the Great Event to begin its experience. It can begin *now.* It is only a matter of bringing the spiritual world into focus.

In *God's Final Effort,* we offer the example of a stereogram, a flat picture which, when we focus properly, becomes three dimensional.

Enter the REAL World

During the moment of the Great Event, the spiritual world will come into focus for each of us. For some it may be overwhelming. For that very reason, why not begin to bring the spiritual world into focus *now*? It requires only a simple act of the mind and soul.

Many of us have had the spiritual world in focus at special times, in special places—times and places of awareness of God. This awareness that Someone is listening when we pray should not be occasional. This awareness can and should be a constant experience.

The world we touch and see with bodily senses has only contingent being. Far more real is the world of God Who is Absolute Being. Our nature requires that we live in both worlds, but most of us are aware only of the less real world, perceived with bodily senses.

If we focus our souls, we can enter the three dimensional world of GOD. And that is what the Great Event is all about.

Power Went Out from Him

Most of us, as humbly testified by Father DeGrandis, do not yet experience the power emanating from the Tabernacle. But He is there in all His Power! In all His Love!

Now Jesus gives us the Heart of His Mother, so that *we may have a heart worthy of being enflamed by His Love and lifted in His Power.*

Oh, how sad that so many who love Jesus think that in praising Mary, they diminish praise of Him! How sad to quote Her words, "Do as He tells you," and yet ignore that He gives us the heart of His Mother *so that we may have hearts worthy of Him!*

Father Philip Bebie was moved to speak at great length, in the light of the "Great Event"—the Warning, the Illumination of Conscience—of consecration to the Immaculate Heart.

Will many despair when they see themselves as God sees them? What about the hundreds of thousands, perhaps millions, who in recent times have approached the Eucharist without sufficient frequent confession?

Oh, how they will wish to hide themselves in the Immaculate Heart of the new Eve, their Mother in Grace!

Now is the time to begin.

The Triumph promised at Fatima will be Eucharistic. Before Our Lady brought to the children of Fatima the message of Her Immaculate Heart, an angel taught them to pray: "O Most Holy Trinity, Father, Son, and Holy Spirit, I adore Thee profoundly. I offer Thee the Most Precious Body, Blood, Soul, and Divinity of Jesus Christ, present in all the Tabernacles of the world, in reparation for the outrages, sacrileges, and indifference by which He is offended. By the infinite merits of the Sacred Heart of Jesus and the Immaculate Heart of Mary, I beg the conversion of poor sinners."

CHAPTER NINETEEN

THE FIRST STEP TO VICTORY

Place the hearts of millions in Our Lady's Heart

When Bishop Ahr died in 1993, with the attendant circumstances described in the second last chapter, we seemed to burst forth with the pent-up message of involvement of the laity in the life of the Church. In 1995, we published the book *You, Too, Go into My Vineyard*.

Five books followed: *NOW the Woman Shall Conquer, The Day I Didn't Die, Too Late?, God's Final Effort*, and this present book which is like a sequel to the last two.

Too Late?

Our Lady had appeared to teenagers in Rwanda and in the former Yugoslavia with a message of warning.

She spoke of a river of blood, bodies without heads, etc., and gave conditions for avoiding what would happen if Her message would be ignored. Ten years later, it was too late for Rwanda and too late for Bosnia, parts of Croatia and Serbia, and Kosovo. Hundreds of thousands perished in a river of blood.

We were inspired to write the book *Too Late?* especially because of the words which hundreds of witnesses heard one of the visionaries of Rwanda say to Our Lady:

"We know what makes you sad. It is because people will not listen until it is too late." And, Our Lady then said She came not only for Rwanda and Africa but for the entire world. She said: "The world is on the edge of catastrophe."

God's Final Effort

Just after that book came off the press, the day Padre Pio was beatified on May 2, 1999, I was wondering: "Is it probably too late for the world? Is the annihilation of several entire nations, of which Our Lady spoke both at Fatima and at Akita, no longer avoidable?"

I seemed to hear Blessed Padre Pio say: *"Look at Fatima in the context of history."* That very day, I began to write *God's Final Effort*.

I was amazed to discover what I had never before perceived in the messages of the Sacred Heart to Saint Margaret Mary. Although I had read them many times before, for the first time I saw the important meaning of the words of Our Lord to Sister Lucia of Fatima, *that as the world failed to respond to the message of His Sacred Heart, so it would be with the message of Fatima,* and the consequences would be similar.

In the past three hundred years of history, as Our Lord indicated to Sister Lucia, *we have a vision of our future. We know what must happen if we continue to fail in our response.*

The Triumph

We are approaching the moment of decision which we have dared to hold up to the reader in these pages. It is the moment of "the Great Event." The annihilation of several entire nations hangs in the balance.

Saint Margaret Mary was told that this would be *"God's final effort to wrest mankind from the reign of Satan."*

Since then, He has sent Our Lady over and over, culminating in messages and warnings at Fatima and Akita to implement that effort.

Now there will be a great turning point in what Saint Margaret Mary called "God's Final Effort." It will be the Illumination of Conscience experienced by every man, woman, and child on the earth. It will be a unique moment of God's Mercy. It will be a unique opportunity for mankind.

More than a Miracle

In these pages, we have described the failed reaction to the Great Miracle of Fatima, and the world's indifference to miracles as exemplified by ignoring the miracle which took place in Naples on the day of Padre Pio's beatification. We can see that even miracles may not evoke the response needed to divert mankind from its path to self-destruction.

Among those present at the miracle of the sun in 1917, which has been called "the greatest miracle in history" and "the greatest event since Pentecost," was a correspondent for one of the major News Services. The next day, as reported by Walsh in his book *Our Lady of Fatima*, "he cabled a long and impressive story about the miracle. But it was never published. Chicago and New York were in the middle of the World Series (baseball), and the long despatch became a one-inch item relegated to page 24, literally snowed under the details of singles, errors, batting averages, and home runs."

The Great Event

The now anticipated "Great Event," the Illumination of Conscience foretold by Blessed Anne Marie Taigi and others, can be expected to accomplish what miracles could not. God's "final effort" will have a never-before-tried impetus touching everyone on earth.

Should we not dare to believe that it will succeed?

Should we not dare to believe that Our Lady did not come to promise the Triumph of Her Heart over a world of burned out corpses? Should we not dare to hope that God's final effort to wrest mankind from the dominion of Satan by the Love of the Sacred Hearts will succeed?

As we say in this book, much has changed in just the last few years before the new millennium. There has been a revolution in communications. Satellites make images and messages instantly available all over the globe.

We are almost ready for the Great Event.

Hearts in the Scales of Justice!

In all three of those last books mentioned above (which it would be helpful for the reader to have read in sequence), we have stressed the importance of consecration to the Sacred Heart of Jesus and the Immaculate Heart of Mary. At the same time, we have suggested a simple way to bring about a worldwide response.

We have suggested worldwide acts of consecration to the Sacred Hearts by the simple means of gathering *signatures to be placed in the Immaculate Heart of Mary as a 2000th birthday gift to Jesus* as an ongoing project timed for, but not limited to, the year 2000.

First Step

The longest journey begins with the first step. And the first step to the Triumph indicated in the message of Fatima is consecration to the Immaculate Heart of Mary.

A first step has to be something real, *a step we know we can take.* Each one of us, if only by obtaining a few names, can be part of it.

On the journey to the Triumph of God in all hearts in the world, we are taking a first real step when we ask our neighbors to sign their names to be placed in the heart of a statue at the sanctuary-museum complex of the Queen of the World at Fatima.

This practical idea came to Mrs. Helen Bergkamp, of Wichita, Kansas, on a visit to Ars, France. She was inspired on seeing a statue of Our Lady on which Saint John Vianney had placed a locket over Our Lady's Heart containing the names of all his parishioners.

The Bishop of Wichita, Helen's brother, offered to be Spiritual Director of the campaign which followed.

A large statue was made with *a recess inside the heart to receive computer discs.* It was enshrined in the Queen of the World center at the Fatima Castle and a movement was begun throughout the world to place *fifty million names in Our Lady's Heart.* (The first thousands were from Great Britain and the U.S. Two million were pledged the first year from the Philippines alone.) *These names will join the more than five million who have already signed the petition for the fifth Marian dogma which, like the collegial consecration of 1984, will be the sign of a great victory in God's final effort to wrest mankind from the reign of Satan.*

The Sacred Hearts invite us to place the names of relatives, friends, and neighbors in Our Lady's Heart, to be offered to the Sacred Heart at this critical moment of God's final effort to withdraw mankind from the reign of Satan.

That final effort began in 1673. After three hundred years of failure to respond to this message from

Heaven, after the bloodiest century in history as a result of our failure to respond, it is now a message which has become, in the words of Pope John Paul II: *"the alternative to mankind's self destruction."*[36]

Moment of Decision

Sign-up sheets may be obtained from the Queen of the World Center, PO Box 20870, Wichita, KS 67208. www.heartofmary.org, e-mail: names@heartofmary.org

Names can be sent by fax, regular mail, or e-mail. They will all be transferred to computer disks and sent to the Queen of the World Center, Ao Castelo, Ourem, Portugal, e-mail: FATIMAREGINAMUNDI@netc.pt

As we said above, this is a first step. Indeed, it may be the first of man's most important journey since he was expelled from the garden of Eden. Placing millions of names in Our Lady's Heart for Jesus will be a giant step to the ultimate Triumph.

It is something we can do *now*.

At the same time, let us not forget all the other necessary ways to make the Triumph a reality, and to hasten it. Let us do as Our Lady commanded: *"Mobilize the laity."* We are ALL needed. At the moment of the Great Event, we must be ready to act. We will be needed to evangelize our brethren throughout the world as never before.

It is the moment of God's great mercy. It is the moment of decision.

---

[36] Letter to Fatima, published in *Osservatore Romano*, October 1, 1997.

AFTERWORD

TWO CROWNS

The prophecies and signs of the Triumph

In the early morning hours of the vigil of the anniversary of the miracle of the sun (the last of the 20th century), the statue of Our Lady, on the front of the Basilica of Fatima, seemed to shine out of the darkness more than usual because the illuminated cross on a crown above the tower, which normally shone more brightly than the statue, was dark. It was hidden by curtained scaffolding.

While actually gazing at that floodlighted statue on the Fatima Basilica, wondering how to write this book, the writing began. And the very day it was finished,[37] *the curtain on the scaffolding above the statue was removed.* There, at the top of the tower, *the crown,*

---

[37] October 14, 1999, the day the first rough draft was finished. Refinement for publication took additional months.

which symbolized the ultimate Triumph of Our Lady as Queen of the World, *shone in a covering of pure gold.*

Fulfilled Vow

The inspiring story behind that covering of gold provides a proper afterword to all that was said in this little book. It also explains the design on its front cover.

An artist who escaped from Poland during the Communist persecution had made a promise to Our Lady. He vowed that when he would have earned enough money, *in thanksgiving for his escape, he would cover the dome of a Marian Shrine, somewhere in the world, in gold.*

He successfully emigrated to America. After many fruitful years, he was ready to keep his vow. On a visit to the Queen of the World Center at the Fatima Castle, he asked the director, Carlos Evaristo, which shrine he should choose for his gift.

Since the crown on the top of the spire of Fatima had been darkened by more than fifty years of exposure to the elements, without a moment of hesitation, the director suggested this Shrine of Fatima, where Pope Pius XII *had crowned Our Lady Queen of the World,* and where a Polish Pope (who called this "the Marian Capital of the world") had brought *the bullet* which almost took his life on May 13, 1981 *to be placed in Our Lady's crown.*

Little Signs

The sight of that shining gold crown on the day this book was finished caused me to exclaim: "Hail, Holy Queen! Thank you for getting me through the task of affirming your Triumph!"

I had seen that crown on the top of the tower of the Basilica of Fatima for the first time over half a century earlier (1946). It was dull bronze even then. But even without a covering of pure gold, it seemed prophetically significant. It seemed to affirm the new era promised here at Fatima by the Queen of the World, the era of the Triumph.

The unveiling of the crown on the day I finished this book seemed meaningful because I began to write it while gazing at the statue on the facade of the Basilica, when the top of the tower was enclosed in curtained scaffolds. And now, after more than fifty years, the great crown above Father McGlynn's towering image of the Immaculate Heart shone, covered in pure gold *as an act of thanksgiving by a refugee from atheistic communism.*

Is it naive to see signs of the Triumph in such little signs: The bullet in the crown of the statue of Our Lady of Fatima *which the forces of atheism fired at the Pope*—the gold on the crown of the tower fulfilling the vow of one *who escaped from the Communist terror*—fulfilling his vow with gold on Our Lady's crown at Fatima when Poland itself was now free?

Such little signs seem to give reassurance *that Heaven keeps Its promises, that the tide has turned.* Mary comes as Our Lady of All Nations to guide the world to Jesus, Who sends the Holy Spirit, and together, They bring us to the Father. One day, like Jesus and Mary, in this world now so sullied, we will live in His Divine Will.

For some, it has already happened.

Dazzling Insights

In the recommended reading which follows is a new book on the "new and divine" holiness referred to by Pope John Paul II in chapter 18—*What Will The Triumph Be?*.

Many may be confused by the various prophecies of purification which may be necessary before the Triumph. Father Bebie said: "The Era of Peace can arrive very soon." But he wondered if there would be sufficient response to make that possible.

Father Bebie said that very soon after the Great Event, very soon after the Illumination of Consciences of individuals throughout the entire world, "the conversion of the world could be so effective that the Era of Peace will come without delay."

However, he added sadly: "Perhaps more likely (given our poor response to the messages from the Hearts of Jesus and Mary), it may take many hard years."

Personal Response So Important!

If the response to the Great Event is not effective, we may see the annihilation of entire nations. Our Lady said at Akita that the good as well as the bad would be consumed. (The "good" who do not respond to Her requests are also responsible.) But *with EACH heart now consecrated to the Immaculate Heart of Mary, the positive effect of the Great Event is increased.* That is why we have stressed over and over that we must begin our response NOW.

Saint Faustina, who lived the "new and divine" holiness, one day asked Our Lord that ALL the persons in the world who died that day would be saved. And Our Lord granted her request!

Our Lady told us to pray after each decade of the Rosary to Jesus; "Lead ALL souls to Heaven." Our Lady would not teach us to say a prayer that could not be answered.

We must not underestimate the power of our prayers, especially from hearts united to the Immaculate Heart to which God can refuse nothing.

If enough of us do not respond, many voices remind us at this moment of the alternative.

Great Events to Come

Rev. Venard Poslusney, O.Carm., in a 1999 Christmas letter ushering in the new millennium,[38] quoted Father Ianuzzzi's *The Triumph of God's Kingdom in the Millennium and End Times* (as in our last chapter) and said:

"We will have a First General Judgment of God upon all mankind (the Illumination of Conscience). It will invite us to repent and come back to God, our Father, *and be renewed in a Second Pentecost.*" He adds:

"During this time, the enemies of God and of all Christians will instigate a persecution that will challenge us to give up our faith or pay a heavy price. The Judgment will be sudden and unexpected, in a 'day' or an 'hour.' After the purification, there will be a long period of blessed peace and renewal for all who have remained faithful to God. Jesus will reign over the earth, not in a visible presence but in the Eucharist. It will be a time of intense and fervent devotion to Christ in the Eucharist."

This new era will be a time of very great saints.

Prophecies of Garabandal

To avoid the impression of anticipating the judgment of the Church concerning the apparitions and messages of Garabandal, we have spoken of the Illumination of Conscience as prophesied by Blessed Anne Marie Taigi and others, independently of the clear message of Garabandal. But it seems fitting, in this afterword, to give more details.

---

[38] Father Venard, eighty-two years of age at the time of this letter, is a Carmelite specialist in mysticism. He has been highly respected by this writer during an acquaintance of more than fifty years.

Dr. J. A. Dominguez,[39] also in an end-of-the-century letter, wrote:

"When I first heard the prophecy of the "Warning" at Garabandal, Spain, it seemed to me humanly impossible. But as we approached the new millennium, fears being expressed seemed to have much in common with this prophecy."

"Something extraordinary will appear in the firmament that everyone in the world will be able to see. Scientists will agree that it is something not normal or ordinary.

"Most important: Everyone on earth will see his or her sins as God does.

"At Fatima, tens of thousands (up to 100,000 according to a scientist who was present) saw a Great Miracle. The Warning will be experienced by *everyone*. It will prepare the world for another Great Miracle at Garabandal."

These prophecies of Garabandal are related in detail in the book, *The Warning*, from which we have quoted in these pages only the parts directly related to the Illumination of Conscience.

Picture on Our Cover

On the front cover of this book is the twelve-star-crown of the Woman of the Apocalypse over a gold crown (like the one on the tower of the Fatima Basilica and on the Fatima statue containing the bullet which struck Pope John Paul II).

---

[39] Author of 68 books and 34 pamphlets with M.D. from the University of Salamanca, and Ph.D. from Albert Einstein College of Medicine in New York. He can be contacted at www.biblia.com or by writing to Box 240, New York, NY 10032. Dr. Dominguez is perhaps one of the best informed persons in the world on the apparitions and messages of Garabandal.

On the back cover we have depicted the actual flag of Europe as it was designed from the Medal of the Immaculate Conception (the "Miraculous Medal"), and as it is displayed at the borders of fifteen nations with the name of the individual country inside the circle of twelve gold stars on a background of solid blue. (A sixteenth nation is now seeking the honor of using this same "Marian" flag, and it is a nation predominantly Muslim!)

However, in the center of the flag on our back cover is shown, *instead of the name of a nation, the symbol of the Triumph: The giving of our hearts to the Immaculate Heart of Mary to be made one with the Sacred Heart of Jesus.*

By placing millions of names in Our Lady's Heart for Jesus we can hasten the ultimate Triumph.

We can do it now.

Golden crown on the monument of the Queen of the World at the Fatima Castle. Directly opposite, separated from the Castle by a low valley, can be seen the tower of the Basilica of Fatima.

RECOMMENDED READING

The Sacred Heart, speaking to Elizabeth Szanto of the coming Triumph, called it the "era of the Spirit of Love" which will result in a "flood of Grace to be compared to the first Pentecost." Jesus said:

"The unbelieving world, which gradually sinks into darkness, *will experience a grave shock* before it will start to believe." He explained:

"This shock will create *a new world through the strength of faith*. Then, confidence in faith will take root in souls and the face of the earth will be renewed because *there will never have been such a deluge of Grace since the Word became Flesh.*"[40]

You have just read some twenty chapters about the shock.

Other books are being written about *the coming deluge of Grace* which will be unprecedented since the Incarnation. Hugh Owen, director of the John Paul II Institute of Christian Spirituality, has written *New and Divine—The Holiness of the Third Christian Millennium.*[41]

It is so new that unless Mr. Owen presented it other than through Scripture, Tradition, and by the example of Saints, you might tend to reject it. It is so precious that Jesus told Blessed Dina Belanger that if embraced by all consecrated souls, *"all other souls would be saved."*

---

[40] For this full message, read *Her Glorious Title*, especially chapter 15. The works of Elizabeth Szanto received ecclesiastical approval and are of greatest importance (as we believe to be the case also with the entire book *Her Glorious Title*) for the "new and divine" holiness of the coming era of triumph.

[41] For details contact John Paul II Institute, PO Box 798, Woodstock, VA 22664. Tel/Fax: 540-453-7429. e-mail: howen@shentel.net

Mr. Owen's breakthrough work dazzles us with the spectacle of what is to come.

Two Parts

The first part of Mr. Owen's book presents the new and divine holiness ("which the Holy Spirit wants to confer upon the Church at the dawn of the third millennium") from Scripture and Tradition.

The second part shows how this new era of holiness began to show its light in the seventeenth century with the school of Cardinal de Berulle, then flowered in the twentieth century—beginning with Luisa Picaretta and exemplified in recent saints like Saint Faustina and Blessed Dina Belanger. The author predicts that soon, in this new millennium, it will become universal.

For those who have read some of the works of Luisa Picaretta, Mr. Owen's work will throw new light on the vision of the coming Triumph of the Sacred Hearts.

For those who have never heard of the new and divine holiness, it may seem like an impossible dream...like the lifting of the veil upon the already approaching glorious time when the prayer of two thousand years will be fulfilled: *"Thy Will be done on earth as It is in Heaven."*

Coming Soon

Mr. Owen clearly reveals this new "Era of Peace for mankind" as the era of the outpouring of the Holy Spirit with diffusion of the gift of living in the Divine Will. At the same time, he shows the path to this gift, as presented by the John Paul II Institute of Christian Spirituality:

1) *total abandonment to the Holy Spirit and to His spouse, the Blessed Virgin Mary;*

2) *an intimate identification with the Hearts of Jesus and Mary;*

3) an appreciation for the unique role of the Pope, and the clergy in union with him, in mediating the "new and divine" holiness to the Church and to the world;

4) the full recognition of one's responsibility for participation in the imminent Triumph of the Immaculate Heart of Mary and the Reign of the Sacred Heart in the world.

In the Near Future

He dares to speak of this reign not only as "imminent," but as *"in the near future."*

"Everything said in these pages," Mr. Owen concludes, "can be seen as a 'perfecting' of the gift of faith."

It is a perfecting of faith in the Triumph promised at Fatima, of faith in the Triumph *of God's Will fulfilled on earth as in Heaven*. And, we can dare to believe that *it can begin now, in each of us, if we believe enough to say "Yes" to the great gift God now offers to the world,* the gift of the "new and divine" holiness.

We also recommend careful reading of *God's Final Effort* and *Her Glorious Title* as preparation for the new era.[42] And, please, SHARE your books! Put your name and address on the inside cover and then give them to others to read! You are welcome to share the contents on the internet.

Let's BE the big voice!

---

[42] Both books available from the 101 Foundation.